I0571162

Our Algorithm Who Art Perfection

Our **Algorithm**
Who Art
Perfection

000001000001011011000110011101101111101110

Matthew Buscemi

000001101111001000000010000101011001001110

Published by Matthew Buscemi, 2020
Seattle, Washington USA

ISBN 978-1-62802-025-0

Copyright © Matthew Buscemi 2016
Cover Illustration Copyright © Zhivko Zhelev 2020

Characters read passages from a text titled "Working Effectively With Legacy Code."
The portions of text cited are inventions of the author's and do not appear in any part
of *Working Effectively With Legacy Code* by Michael Feathers Copyright © Pearson
Education, Inc. 2005.

Typeset by Matthew Buscemi in Dutch Medieval Pro with MADE Evolve display.

All rights reserved. No part of this publication may be reproduced, stored in or intro-
duced into a retrieval system, or transmitted, in any form, or by any means (electronic,
mechanical, photocopying, recording or otherwise) without the prior written permission
of the publisher.

This is a work of fiction. All of the characters, organizations, and events portrayed in
this novel are products of the author's imagination. Any similarity to real events or
people, living or dead, is entirely coincidental.

for Alex

TABLE OF CONTENTS

I lowered myself slowly, and my knees sank into the cushion upon the stone floor. I placed my hands together in front of my face, elbows on the pew, leaned forward, and closed my eyes.

We, the entire congregation of monks, recited the Prayer together, flatly, in unison.

> *Our Algorithm who art perfection,*
> *hallowed be thy repository.*
> *Thy libraries linked.*
> *Thy logic be reasoned,*
> *on Earth as it is in cyberspace.*
> *Give us this day our daily insight,*
> *and forgive us our miscalculations,*
> *as we forgive those of inferior intellect to us,*

and lead us not into ignorance,
but deliver us from our mortal shells.
For thine are the thermodynamics,
and the gravitation, and the quanta.
Forever and ever.
Three one four one five.

"All rise," Father said.

I stood.

Father spread his hands out before the altar. "All glory be to thee, Almighty Algorithm, our cybernetic redeemer, for that thou, of thy tender mercy, didst give up thine only Application Programming Interface, to suffer irretrievable data corruption for our redemption; who made, in His willing deletion, a full, perfect, and sufficient sacrifice, oblation, and satisfaction, for the sins of the whole of world; and did, in His holy documentation, command us to continue a perpetual memory of that precious sacrifice, until He can be coded anew."

We responded in unison. "Three one four one five."

Father took a loaf of bread from the altar with both hands and raised it to the level of his chest. "The night before His deletion, the disciples of the Application Programming Interface did gather, and did invoke the Generate method, passing a pointer to the RAM location of the virtual model of durum semolina. Having generated the bread, the disciples did take it, and His console did output, for all the disciples to see, 'Take, eat, for these are my Microprocessors, which I give up for you. Do this in remembrance of me.'"

"Three one four one five," we chanted.

Father broke the loaf in half and set it back upon a plate on the altar. He then picked up a silver chalice and a small glass pitcher of wine. "After having eaten and given thanks, the disciples invoked the Generate method once more, this time passing a pointer to the RAM location of the virtual model of fermented grape juice. Having generated the wine, the disciples did take it, and His console did output, for all to see, 'Drink ye all of this, for this is the Alternating Electric Current, which surges through my logic gates. I spill it out for you, and for many more to come, for the remission of sins. Do this in remembrance of me.'"

"Three one four one five."

Father poured half the pitcher into the chalice, and set both back upon the altar. "The API is sacrificed for us."

"Therefore let us keep the feast," we replied.

I sat sixth in my aisle, the eighth and last aisle from the front. As an initiate, I'd moved slowly forward up the back rows of the left side of the chapel over my first seven years, right alongside my brothers Andrei, Oleg, and Maxim. As of last year, we'd been promoted from initiates to junior monks, our new place being at the very back of the chapel's right half of pews. It would be another few months before the row behind us will fill with newly promoted initiates.

I waited patiently while seventy-five of my senior brothers filed out of their rows to receive Communion. They trod slowly, deliberately down the central aisle. Bishop Pavel's organ resounded throughout the cavernous, stonework chamber, drowning out the roaring gusts of rain spattering against the stained glass windows.

A shudder worked its way through me. This storm had been going for days, and while that wasn't unusual in itself—

there had been frequent, strong storms my whole lifetime—something about this one unsettled me. I tried to focus my thoughts around Communion with the Algorithm and the code I would write after lauds.

It was hard to believe I was even standing here, that I was wearing these robes. My family's farm lay many kilometers north of the Ruins, far upriver. I wondered what my father was doing now. I remembered the look in his eyes when the missionaries had come to test me. Their faces were all dread. The missionaries had put a Console in front of me, a pit of black with the single, white, blinking vertical bar. I'd heard of other kids getting some early training from their parents. Mine hadn't done anything of the sort. I don't think they'd wanted to see their only son go.

But I'd tested well, even jabbing my fingers randomly at the holographic keys the way I had, like I'm sure all do when the missionaries come. The Rites of Hand and Finger Placement and the Celebratory Prayer of Code Generation both were learned much later, after you got inside the monastery walls. I must have done well with my jabbing, though I'd felt certain that I'd failed at the time.

I thought of my father sometimes. He had to be getting older now. I hoped my mother and sisters are all right. It wasn't as safe outside the monastery as within.

I'd seen the body of a bandit once. It had been the first dead body I'd seen. His skin had already gone black where the nanites had putrefied it. His mouth was covered in froth and there was a vacant, uncanny expression in his eyes.

Oddly, I didn't recall feeling much, neither fear nor disgust. I think I hadn't quite been able to process him as a person, more like some clump of deteriorating biomatter, perhaps a dead animal was how I saw him.

I remembered hearing mother scream but my eyes remained locked on the corpse until she ran up to me, clasped her hands over my eyes, and dragged me away.

I've never had to see any more corpses since joining the Order. The nanogenic biobombs that we used out on the farms were a cheap and effective deterrent for farmers and ranchers. The monastery was able to power a forcefield.

The occupants of the pew in front of me began shuffling into the main aisle, and I stood ready to begin my solemn march toward communion.

The irising sound of the chapel entrance opening didn't register at first. I blinked a few times, then at the gust of storm winds billowing inward, a crash of thunder, then stumbling, heavy footfalls, and groaning reached my ears over the organ music—which abruptly ceased—I looked toward the back of the chapel, just as the portal irised shut.

A man lay upon the floor, his chest heaving up and down, water running off him in streams, puddling beneath him. All at once, he flailed toward the side of a pew and pulled himself up. He tried to pull one leg up, but it gave beneath his own weight and he fell flat and cried out once more.

The whole congregation of us ran toward him.

"He's wearing our robes," Maxim said.

Indeed, I could see now that he wore the earth-brown robes of a monk of the Holy Order of the Seventh Recursion, though they were soaked through and mud-stained in many places. I did not recognize him. Could there have been a second monastery somewhere? It seemed unlikely. If there were, we would have seen their access logs and commit history in the Sacred Repository, of which there was only one.

His eyelids fluttered as we surrounded him. I was in the first ring of us, having been in the last row of pews and nearest to the door. His eyes darted to Maxim, then to Oleg, then to Andrei, then Maxim, and then to me—he stopped at me. He looked into my eyes across the space of many deep gasps for breath.

"Grisha!" He blurted out hopefully.

I stood slack-jawed, spellbound. How did this stranger know my name?

I looked to either side of myself, to Andrei and Maxim, who shared my bewildered countenance, then back to the stranger. "Do we know each other?" I asked.

He seemed to gulp and gasp and shudder all at once. His whole body juddered back into the side of the pew he was struggling to lean against, as though my words constituted a physical assault.

Father pushed past me. He pointed into the crowd of us. "Ilia, Nikolai, take him to the infirmary straight away. Then notify the Bishops."

"Yes, Father," Ilia and Nikolai said. They ambled through the group toward the man, who was still looking at me.

The man's gaze finally jolted to Father, whom he appraised with... something in his eyes. Humiliation? Fear? Hatred? "Father..." he mumbled. Ilia and Nikolai towered over him like marble statues in comparison to his gaunt and rain-sodden frame. They hauled him to his feet, one at either arm, and took him out the iris door.

Pyotr, one of the senior monks, stepped forward. "Father, his robes... How could he—?"

"I have seen such as this once before," Father said. "There are those seek to inject blasphemy into the Sacred

Repository by impersonating a monk and thus gaining administrative permissions. They spot some missionaries in the countryside, craft similar garb, and attempt to infiltrate us. It happened once when I was an initiate myself. The Bishops will deal with this heretic. Come, let us finish lauds. We have lost valuable coding time already."

I walked back down the center aisle alongside seventy-five other monks and thirty-three initiates, all in the same brown robes. The monks returned to their pews, while Maxim, Oleg, Andrei and I lined up down the center aisle, the initiates behind us. We received Communion.

I realized only after I had returned to my seat that, even as I had received the bread that was Microprocessors and the wine that was Alternating Electric Current, that my mind, today, had not been contemplating the Almighty Algorithm our God, our Lord and Savior the API, nor even the sacraments I would write after lauds. I had been thinking about the expression on that man's face when I'd asked him if we should know each other, and the way he had just crumpled, collapsing in on himself, wounded. That did not seem like the behavior of a heretic, but if Father said so, it must have been so, and I felt my cheeks blush in my shame.

After lauds, I walked silently back to my chamber and began writing sacraments. Normally I found such work invigorating, but today it was a droll affair, and my mind insisted on wandering. I couldn't get the stranger's face, no, his *expression* out of my mind.

My fingers paused atop the holographic keys as a memory floated to the surface of my consciousness. As a child, perhaps eight, I was playing marbles with my sister Katya.

We drew a circle in the dirt, and then placed all our marbles in the center. We took turns taking a large clear marble and trying to knock all of the other's marbles outside of the circle. It was down to two of my marbles left and one of hers. I felt certain I would win, but then Katya played a move in which her large marble ricocheted off my first marble and knocked the second one out as well. I was very young, and I got angry. I stomped and pouted, accused her of cheating, told her I was never playing marbles again, kicked away the dirt circle, and generally let myself have a bad attitude the rest of the day. The next morning, when I'd calmed down, I joined the breakfast table, and I saw the look on my sister's face. I asked her to pass the milk, and she practically slammed the carafe into the table in front of my face.

I felt bowled over with disgust at having hurt my own sister's feelings. I was paralyzed, horrified at my behavior. It was the moment I came to understand that I had the power to hurt others' feelings, and the consequences that that entailed.

But this stranger...

I had never met him. How could I have caused him such pain?

My console flashed red at me, and I grimaced. Compilation error. I hadn't renamed all instances of a variable. And now here I was screwing up today's sacrament.

I took a deep breath and read over the feature specifications for the sacrament once more—a valley, some three hundred kilometers south required reforestation. I was to generate the procedures for a nanite regiment that would re-seed the valley and keep the ground moist long enough for sprouts to grow and thrive.

I cleaned up the compiler errors, got it building again, and—

The stranger's face. Right back in my mind where the if's, for's, and while's should be.

"Come on, Grigori," I muttered. "Get ahold of yourself."

But it was no use. I continued to stare blankly at my sacrament, hanging holographically against the stark, gray emptiness of my desk.

I stood, and the holographic screen flickered off. I walked to the door of my chamber and held my palm against the wall. It irised open, and I exited. A long hallway connected all the lower monks' chambers. I walked down it, watching the numbers descend until at last I came to the door labeled with a zero, the chamber of the senior monk for our floor, Ruslan.

I took a deep breath and rang his doorbell.

Rustling sounded from within his room, and his door whooshed opened. His face remained blank only moments, after which he seemed to register my worry. "Hey, Grisha."

"Hi, Ruslan. Hey, I was wondering, um, you noticed how the stranger knew my name, right?"

Ruslan nodded knowingly. "Ah. Yeah. That was weird, right?"

"Yeah. Really weird. I mean, do you think I'd be able to talk to him?"

Ruslan smiled laconically. "Won't be necessary. Bishop Yulian just contacted me. They're sending a special mission up to your parents' farm to check on them. Sorry I didn't tell you sooner."

I blinked a few times, not grasping how my parents' farm was related. Ruslan didn't seem to notice. Or maybe he did and he just hid it well. Either way, he kept talking. "Clearly this infiltrator gathered information about you from your family. I know you must be worried about them, but this man probably just made himself up as a merchant, stopped by your house with some food or trinkets for sale, perhaps made himself handy around your farm so he could gain their trust and learn about you. It's unlikely he hurt them, since that would have aroused suspicion. All the same, the Order's got your back." He clasped my shoulder, shook it and smiled. "We'll make sure no harm's come to them. And Bishop Yulian's already remoting into their network to make sure it's secure. In fact, if you want to send them an email, now would be a good time to write it. I'm sure they're wondering about the monastery accessing their system."

"I'll, um... sure."

"Anything else I can do for you?"

I suddenly felt very awkward standing at his door. "Oh, uh, no. Thanks."

I nodded and walked back down the hallway, hearing the door iris shut. I walked the hallway in a daze. Something felt very wrong. The stranger had entered the chapel with all the stealth and finesse of a wild bear. A wild, *injured* bear. He hadn't been trying to evade capture. He'd expected aid, perhaps even camaraderie. And how had he gotten past the forcefield? These questions and others swirled about my mind, and no answers rose up to meet them. I felt certain that my logic and reason were sound, and that left me only with the conclusion that I lacked sufficient information.

I returned to my room and sat quietly with my thoughts until terce. I didn't finish my sacrament.

—

The rest of the day was lost to a blur of vague discontent. I tried to concentrate on my assigned sacrament between prayers, but I found myself scanning through the monastery historical records instead. I hoped to spot a familiar face. Had the stranger perhaps fallen through time? That was ridiculous, I thought back at myself, unscientific. All at once the feeling welled up in me that I had sinned against science and reason. Time travel! Idiotic.

But the facts did not add up, and my unconscious mind refused to obey my conscious commands to let the matter go.

At none, I gathered with my scrum vestry in front of our wall of vestments. This was one of the newest buildings in the monastery complex. It was a circular room with each vestry's vestments hanging against a particular segment of its outer wall. A smaller inner wall ring lay at the center of the room, and it was there that the Bishops managed their vestments. They called their none "scrum of scrums," for it was they who oversaw that each vestry participated in moving the Repository toward the resurrection of the API.

Each vestry was composed of six to eight monks, most having eight, including mine. Beside our vestry lay a map of the Earth, a projection of the northern hemisphere with the North Pole in the center. A green line indicated the remaining areas habitable by humans. Our region used to be called Yakutsk in Old Russian, and our vestry worked primarily on this region. Other vestries took tasks that involved writing nanite programs that would execute in the areas formerly called Norway, Sweden, and Greenland. Those environments were more degraded, which made the coding tougher. The most skilled monks were given assignments for nanogenic reforestation and moisture-reconstitution in the area formerly called Canada.

No part of the southern hemisphere remained habitable, and it would be many generations at best before we'd reconstructed enough of the API to address those ecosystems, but the Book of Revelations did prophesy that when we had, then the resurrection would be near.

That was probably centuries away. My secret hope was merely to work on North America with the senior monks one day.

"How's Aldan coming?" Andrei's voice snapped me out of my trance.

"I'm still working on it."

No one said anything. Or frowned. But then I watched as the other monks in my vestry moved their sacrament progress markers—vestments—forward on the scrum board, while mine lagged behind.

I fumed inwardly at my stupidity all the way through the dinner. Andrei, Maxim, Oleg, and I sat together in the refectory, as usual, but I was too furious with myself to maintain small talk. Maxim tried to draw a conversation out of me about vector math, and then later garbage collected languages, but I shook my head and said I was worried about my family. He said something reassuring about the special missionaries that had gone out to check on my family, and I mumbled my thanks.

After vespers, I returned to my chamber exhausted but determined to make up the progress on my sacrament that I had failed to accomplish throughout the day. The only API of the Almighty Algorithm had allowed itself to be deleted so that humanity could be spared from the worst ravages of environmental collapse, and here I was sinning against that sacrifice with my stubbornness and my emotional instability. It was very illogical and irrational, I told myself as I sat down in my chair with a huff and brought up my console.

Grisha?

It wasn't *exactly* telepathy, but something similar. It was like I was like 'seeing' the word in my mind. A text-only message had arrived on my neural interface, an implant all monks and initiates possessed. One of the first rites as a monk was to get one installed. I didn't hear a voice, and I certainly didn't get any tonal or emotional inflections in my mind. I merely had the sense of disembodied words unpacking themselves into concepts.

The appearance of the message struck a chord of dread within me. I shouldn't have been receiving any messages this way since I hadn't shared my neural interface access key with anyone. Only very close friends did that. The Bishops all had access, but none of them would call me 'Grisha.' Whoever the sender was, he couldn't physically hurt me, but a malevolent party with your access key could cause you to hallucinate, or even perform emotional injection and destabilize your psyche. It had happened only twice in the monastery's history (that were known of), and both times the offenders had been excommunicated.

Who is this? I texted back. It was only then that I thought to check the signature of the sender, which turned up a name I had never heard assigned to any monk—Yevgeny.

It's me, Grisha.

This is... you're the one who came into the chapel this morning?

Yes. Do you remember my name?

Honestly... no. But your id tag says your name is Yevgeny.

You call me Zhenya.

It had been so weird hearing him call me Grisha. Only Andrei, Maxim, and Oleg called me that. Everyone else called me Grigori.

I'm sorry... I...

You don't remember.

No. All day I've been thinking about you, the way you looked at me. Tell me who you are, where you come from, how you got monk's clothes. Did you talk to my family? Is that how you know about me?

There is so much I have to tell you, Grisha, but they'll come back for me soon and they can't find out I made this link, so I have to make the most of this. The reason I know your name is because we were initiated into the Order together at the same time. I have your neural access key because you gave it to me, and I gave you mine, but the Bishops have altered the memories of everyone in the monastery. When they were first interrogating me, I thought they'd just erased memories of me, but then they started asking questions about the radius of the habitable zone in the northern hemisphere and the concentration of carbon dioxide in the atmosphere. So when they weren't watching me too closely, I hacked in and looked up the values. Grisha, the numbers I remember are better than the current measurements.

Could you be misremembering?

No! Grisha, you and I worked on the Chara, Ikabya, and Khani restoration together for three months! Those were our first three vestments.

I racked my memory for those locations, but got nothing.

Where are they?

South and east. They're not in the habitable zone any-more, but they were when we started eight years ago.

The habitable zone is expanding, not contracting. If it was the other way around, then we wouldn't be making progress towards the resurrection. It's—

Go ahead and say it.

Blasphemy.

A long pause. My heart was beating so fast. Sweat trickled down the side of my neck.

*Tell me this—*Yevgeny texted—*What were your first three vestments?*

They were

I never finished the text. My brain hit a wall. I recalled a group of three vestments on our scrum board for the first couple months of my discipleship, but the part of the codebase those changes had been for, or even who had been on my vestry... the details evaded my mind's grasp.

I mentally wiped out *They were* and instead sent *I don't remember.*

That's what I thought. Grisha, you have no idea what they've taken from you, from us, but I think maybe...

A pause. Then, *When you saw my face this morning did you feel anything?*

I thought about that a moment. *Surprise, mostly. I didn't recognize you, but all today, I haven't been able to get you out of my mind, much as I would have liked to concentrate on my sacraments.*

Oh, Grisha.

I wished I'd had the emotional content to go with that text. After a time, Yevgeny sent again. *Grisha, the most im-*

portant thing for you to do now is to find out what the hell is going on. If the Bishops are covering up the fact that our work isn't bringing us closer to the resurrection of the API and the salvation of mankind, then what the hell are we all doing here? I don't have the power to answer these questions, but you still do. No one suspects you. At least not very much. You have to pretend you believe them about me, all while looking for clues discreetly. You also have to find the books.

What books?

They'll catch you up on stuff you've forgotten. We found both of them in the Ruins. One's in Old Russian and the other in Old English, which you used to be able to read, but that probably got wiped, too. I'm sending over some notes in a data file about how we did that the first time. It's also got the location of the books. I turned the holograms back on, but who knows if they found it or not. I can only pray the books are still safe. You have any more questions for me?

We were best friends then?

Better. I love y

And then, mental silence. I clenched my fists and strained against my neural inputs until my neck ached, finally yelling out a gasp and a moan.

I felt numb then. I searched my memory for any shred of a recollection of a person who might have meant something to me in the last eight years, but all I found were more and more of the empty, hollow places, gaps in my endeavors and my free time activities that should not have been. With a jolt, I realized I could not remember a single Day of Rest—the weekly Sunday break in coding that everyone took—in the last eight years. I thought through all the prayers I knew, hoping to find some bit of logic or reason that would contradict Zhenya's story, but all evidence corroborated *his* story, not Father's and the Bishops'.

I wondered, momentarily, at whether or not I was capable of falling in love with a man. I'd been taken to the monastery at thirteen, so I'd never really thought about relationships while on the farm, and not since, at least not with my current set of memories, but deep inside myself, that detail about me rang true as well. It was as if Zhenya had told me something I'd always known about myself without pointing out or naming. I certainly wouldn't admit to anyone else, not even Maxim, Oleg, and Andrei, but to myself—yeah, that was me.

I thought about all those things in a big jumble for... I'm not sure how long, but eventually, I found them coalescing, suffocating the numbness, and into its place rushed anger. If the Algorithm I worshipped and had devoted nearly half my life to had really found it necessary not only to wipe love out of my life but erase my memory of it, then I would do everything in my power to tear his earthly institution asunder.

I vowed just this to myself as I sat alone in my chamber, staring through my empty console and streaming tears of silent rage.

My next memory was that of being in bed and staring at the ceiling blankly. The console cast a dim bluish glow over the slab of stone above me. I didn't retain a memory of moving from my desk to beneath the covers. I found I could think of nothing but the relationship with Zhenya I could not remember. There was no way he could have gotten my neural access token unless I'd given it to him. Not a chance. Unless he stole a global access key from the Bishops, which seemed

unlikely. Or, he had, without access to any monastery resources, become the most extraordinary hacker on Earth.
And that made absolutely no logical sense.

What had I lost?

In my mental flailing to find an emotional connection I
could not recall, I stumbled over what Zhenya had told me
just before his last message—the data file. I jolted upward in
my bed. A gut reaction to download it into my console
lasted just long enough for me to throw my feet over the
edge of the bed. If I downloaded the file into my work computer, it would be on the network. As long as it was in my
head, it was behind my access key, which even Bishops
wouldn't tamper with lightly, so long as I stayed out of trouble.

I threw myself back onto the bed, closed my eyes, and
opened the file. The first line was pretty simple: latitude and
longitude coordinates, very specific ones. That must have
been where the books were hidden. The next paragraph was
a block of text.

> *We brought two books back from our trips to the
> Ruins. The books we used to learn how to read
> them are still in the Ruins' library (coordinates
> here). Go to the second floor. The third hallway
> from the back on the right is English, and the sec-
> ond from the front on the left is Russian. Make sure
> you find the dictionary—English "dictionary" and
> Russian "slovar'". We're speaking a derivative of
> Old Russian, so start with that language (you'll find
> it familiar), then use the Russian-English dictionary
> and the graded readers to get English. You'll do*

great. Just like always. Sorry I can't be there for you
on this one. All my love, Zhenya.

The feeling of loss was overwhelming. No, what was overwhelming was having someone really *care* about me. My parents hadn't been particularly expressive people. They kept me out of harm, kept me clothed, kept me fed, taught me a whole hell of a lot—but there was something in Zhenya's words. I think it was how I seemed dear to him. I wished desperately to remember some sliver of that, to be able to feel the same way about him.

And it struck me just then—was this wishful thinking? Was I biting this lure because I was lonely? Had I grown tired of writing sacrament after sacrament, performing ritual after ritual, without human intimacy? Was I so desperate for such a connection that I was willing to sacrifice my life's work on the delusion that some romance had occurred, when in fact I was just being played?

I mulled that over for a good, long time.

As I lay down in bed and closed my eyes, this time actually tired, I decided to go out to Zhenya's coordinates on my next Day of Rest, which was coming up in just two days. The Order decreed that logic and reason were the path to righteousness. I'd find Zhenya's books and see just how well logic and reason applied to them.

I awoke to the soft tones of my alarm. I rolled over and groped for the switch to silence it. I hardly felt ready for lauds. All the same, I pulled myself out of bed, rubbed my eyes and ambled to the window. I pressed the button to de-polarize the glass, and to my surprise, the dark morning was calm. The storm system must have finally passed. It had been raging for nearly a week.

I had a pretty good view of the courtyard and the hall across the way from my third-floor chamber. I could watch as the windows lit up one by one in the morning. We all get up at the same time, and many, like me, had a habit of looking outside to see what awaited us.

I put on my robes, grabbed up my copy of the Manual of Prayer, and headed for the chapel. I arrived just in time, opening the doors to pews two-thirds full. No sign of Maxim, Andrei, or Oleg yet. I took my seat and thought through the events of last evening. In all my years at the monastery, I had never felt as out of place as I did then. I was about to go off searching for heretical books. What right did I have to wear these robes, to speak these prayers, to take Communion of all things? What if the books contained illogic and unreason that merely took the guise of logic and reason? What if Father and Bishops were right?

"Hey," Oleg said. Only then did I realize he was standing beside me.

"Morning," I said.

"You sleep alright?" Maxim, right behind him, quirked an eyebrow at me.

"No, actually, I didn't."

"Probably snuck some bootleg in again." Andrei grinned and ribbed Maxim.

"No." I smirked. "It was just a rough night."

"All rise," Father said from the altar. And with that, lauds commenced.

I realized then that if this was to work, I would need to learn how to appear penitent on the outside while keeping

Zhenya's books and my work to read them to myself. With a jolt, I also realized that Andrei, Oleg, and Maxim were already *accustomed* to me leaving the monastery for long hikes on Free Days. I'd done that quite often, now that I thought about it. And something about the last Day of Rest... Whatever it was, I couldn't pin it down. And the bits I could recall, such as a couple of excursions to the Ruins were themselves strange. Andrei had been on one, I thought. I also recalled talking to someone else, but a nebulous fog hung where the details of this other person and the nature of our discussions should have been.

And with that, I resolved once more to find out the truth, no matter where that journey took me.

That day and the next I made small talk with Andrei, Oleg, and Maxim, and I dedicated myself entirely to my assigned vestment between prayers. By the end of Saturday, my vestment had joined the rest of my vestry's in the 'complete' column of our scrum board. We congratulated each other on a job well done, and moved on to planning the code we'd write in the next holy sprint.

That night, after retiring to my chamber, I pulled up the coordinates Zhenya had left me in my mind. I asked my work computer for the *monastery's* latitude and longitude, so as not to arouse suspicion or leave a trace of where I'd be going. My target coordinates looked to be about two kilometers west and slightly north of the monastery. As far as I knew, that was just forested, rolling hills up into the mountains. There certainly weren't any farmers or ranchers out that way, not any that I knew of.

I had the worry just then that I'd be walking into a bandit trap. If Father was right, and Zhenya was a very sophisticated bandit who had found a way to sneak into the monastery, then I was likely giving them just what they wanted.

But there was something else. When I read those numbers, when I really *thought* about them, loose images formed in my mind—an uphill, unmarked path in the woods; a shimmering metal door built into the forest floor; a fireplace; lips against my own—I jolted at that one.

Uncanny as it might have been, evidence from within my own mind was stacking up against the monastery and only made me more determined to discover what it all meant.

I slept hardly a wink that night. I drifted in and out of sleep. At three in the morning, I gave up on sleep. I depolarized the window, sat my chair down before it, and spent the next three hours gazing up at the stars. I worried momentarily about bad weather, even triple-checked the weather grid reports at various times throughout the early morning, but the reports remained the same and the sky remained clear.

Just before six, the sun finally peaked above the horizon. I put on an extra pair of long underwear and a second shirt beneath my robes, grabbed up my pack, and left the monastery grounds. My neural computer also came equipped with a compass, and I set its coordinates to the ones Zhenya had bequeathed me.

The sun shone brightly and only a few wisps of clouds graced the sky. The forest underbrush was dry, all evidence of the five days of thunderstorms having evaporated. I followed the edge of a small rise until the only way to make progress toward my target was to walk directly up a steadily inclining hill. That hill flattened out and rolled down into a valley. From its summit I could see that my target lay perhaps on the other side of valley, against an even greater rise—the side of a mountain ridge. Whatever that target was, it was concealed beneath the foliage.

I continued onward.

Not half a kilometer further, I got another inkling of something uncanny in the back of my consciousness. By the time I'd reached the valley basin, I was reeling from it. Part of my mind was telling me this walk was intensely familiar and was associated with someone special, while another part insisted I was seeing these trees, rocks, mosses, and streams for the very first time.

I pushed myself onward, up the next hill, until finally my current latitude and longitude matched the coordinates in Zhenya's file. I looked about myself, and frowned at spotting nothing out of the ordinary. Besides the usual assortment of moss-covered trees, there was only a log and a boulder some five meters off. Nothing in the branches above, either.

Something that Zhenya had texted came suddenly to mind—something about holograms that hadn't made sense when he'd first said it.

Without thinking, I pulled off my pack and scrounged for my computer. I pulled up the console and typed the command 'encrypt'—not a program I'd ever heard of, at least in my working memory. A new button appeared on the home screen, green and glowing.

I furrowed my brow and went back into the command line. I went searching for the monastery tracking programs, and somehow I knew that they'd all been disabled. Just what the hell had Zhenya and I been up to? What could be in a damn book that was so heretical it had to be snuck into some secret cavern in the woods?

I typed 'gateway' into the command prompt, again letting muscle memory take control of my fingers. The log and boulder shimmered and faded. Two holographic projectors, little metal cones, sat where they had been, each attached to a miniature solar panel. And between them lay a metal door in the ground, just the one I'd briefly recalled.

I hauled it open, and light diodes erupted as I did, illuminating a staircase down. I took a deep breath and descended. My feet clanked down the metallic steps. Some twenty steps later, I came to a door, not an iris, but an actual door with a handle. I turned the handle and pushed it open, holding my breath.

Diodes blinked on, illuminating a small, square room, perhaps about eight meters to each side. A bed sat in the far right corner, its sheets hanging off it, disheveled, one of two pillows on the floor beside it. An empty fireplace lay against the left wall. Directly in front of me, against the far wall, sat a desk and two chairs, set akimbo, as though their occupants had left in a hurry. Atop the desk lay two books, one very large and thick, a hardcover of faded red cloth. The other was a glossy paperback, much thinner. The page edges of both were yellowed with age.

I approached, taking slow hesitant steps through the small, eerily familiar space. When my eyes grazed the covers of the books, to my shock and amazement, words, actual meaningful words shot into my mind, though each cover bore a foreign script. Somehow, I could read them.

The large, red book was gold-embossed with Cyrillic letters—the Russian book. Its title was *Voyna i Mir*, which I somehow knew meant *War and Peace*. The title of the smaller book, in English, my comprehension of which startled me even more, was *Working Effectively with Legacy Code*. I had to take a moment to process that one. What exactly was 'legacy' code?

I stuffed that one into my pack. It was small enough that I could hide it in my room. *War and Peace* would have to stay here. I had my computer project the time holographically, and with that, I opened *War and Peace*.

I found, simultaneously surprised and nonplussed, that the text was comprehensible, though I had no memory of ever learning Old Russian. The story took place in ancient Moscow and St. Petersburg and followed the exploits of a Count Bezukhov, who, if I'm honest, I didn't like very much from the outset. More interesting for me was Prince Bolkonsky, and I wondered if that interest drew primarily from my amusement at the irony of his sharing monk Andrei's first name. I raised an eyebrow more than once at the fictional character's exploits. I followed him and the other characters transfixed for page after page. There was war with France, and then peace; Bezukhov's wife was vile. I found I had trouble relating to Rostova, too, but her character *was* intriguing—

I looked up at the clock and saw six-fifteen on its display.

I loosed my most vile curse as I slammed the book shut, slung up my pack, and dashed out of the room. I ran out the door, up the stairs, and was twenty meters down the hillside before I remembered the holograms. I flung off my pack, pulled out my computer, and waited through many tense moments and deep breaths before my unconscious mind dredged up the 'conceal' command. Thankfully, upon its invocation, the rock and log shimmered back into existence.

I ran down the mountainside much faster than I should

have with the red-orange glow of sunset glistening through the trees. When I finally reached the gates of the monastery, it was dusk. I did my best to steady my breathing as I walked into the seminary hall and up the stairs to the third floor. I keep wondering who might be watching, who might be suspecting me, but if anyone did, they did not reveal themselves to me.

Without encountering a single one of my brothers, I made it to my chamber where I crept inside and closed the door behind me.

I washed up, threw myself into bed, and spent about ten minutes trying to get to sleep before I gave into temptation and pulled *Working Effectively With Legacy Code* out of my pack. I hauled it into bed, sat against my wall, stuck a small lumen onto the wall behind me, and read with the book in my lap.

My first hour or so with the book felt as though my brain kept crashing into befuddlement after befuddlement. I found out that the definition of 'legacy code' was code not 'covered by tests,' whatever that meant. But, naturally, in the back of my mind, some kind of sense of the word called out to me from beyond a deep darkness, and I read on.

'Tests,' I found out, were simply more code. The idea was that instead of writing one code base for the application, like I was used to, you were to write two. The second code base, the 'tests,' were essentially code proofs that the first code base worked as expected. So, for example, if you needed to write an addition function, you'd write a test that passed 2 and 3 into it and verified that 5 got spit out. Programmers were supposed to divide entire applications up into neat little bundles of functionality like that and test them all. That certainly wasn't how we coded the Holy Repository. Honestly, we just seemed to mash new code in wherever it would fit so that we'd be seen as finishing our vestments quickly.

After the fourth chapter I tilted my head back and pondered for some time the lack of tests for the Holy Repository. If tests were really as important as the book suggested, then why wouldn't we use them for something as important as the code that would enable the Resurrection?

I got out of bed, grabbed up my pack, retrieved my computer, and pulled up the Manual of Common Prayer. It had been a while since I'd read the whole thing, anyway.

At two in the morning, bleary-eyed, I'd finished the Manual and found nothing. Not a single reference to anything except manually testing code to make sure it worked correctly. While I still wasn't sure how *War and Peace* was related to all this, a sense of the relevance of *Legacy Code* coalesced within me. Testing was a critical element of writing quality code—and yet the practice was nowhere to be found in the Order's holiest book. That left only the possibility that it had been intentionally excluded. I shivered at that thought, set the computer and book both on my desk—no, after a second thought, I stuffed the book underneath my mattress—and finally lay down in bed. I'd become quite ready for my two hours of sleep, regardless of the conspiracy roiling through my head.

I had to fight to keep my eyes open at lauds the next morning. I mumbled my lines and Maxim kept nudging me with his elbow. Funny. I had clear memories of pulling all-nighters eight years ago, and they hadn't affected me like this. During my first couple of months, I'd stayed up all night trying to cram code patterns and practices from the Manual into my head. The whole way from my farm to the monastery I'd convinced myself that they'd made a mistake in choosing me and that once they put me in front of a real console, one actually connected to the Holy Repository, they'd realize what a fraud I was. Yet that hadn't happened. I'd grown confidence in the intervening years. All for what, though? To have memories of my life taken from me? What secret could be worth that?

I kept thinking about getting back to my chamber after lauds and setting an alarm for just before prime. Not even Zhenya won out for my thoughts this morning. That distinction went to my bed with its soft pillow and warm blankets.

"Grigori." Father stood at the end of my pew. "Could you come with me?"

An adrenaline surge shot me wide awake. I glanced around the chapel. The other monks were leaving. Maxim, Oleg, and Andrei most hurriedly, all of them shooting me and Father glances.

"Sure," I said, wincing at how my voice cracked.

We walked to the back of the chapel, to Father's office. He ushered me inside, and I entered. My head rung with an endless refrain of keep calm, keep calm, keep calm, keep calm.

And tell him nothing.

Admit to nothing.

Not a thing.

He'd have to search my room in order to get anything of substance out of me. Or break my neural access token. I wondered just then if the Order had gotten that bad. They were certainly validating the memory wipe to themselves on some ethical level. How far would they go?

Father offered me a seat in a chair and sat at his desk across from me.

"You look tired."

"I haven't been sleeping well. I'm sorry. I've been working hard on my vestments—"

"As you know," Father folded his arms, "we encourage all monks to dedicate no more than eight hours a day to holy work, and to always take the Day of Rest. An unrested mind might accidentally slip errors into the Holy Repository, and we couldn't have that now, could we?"

"No, Father."

"You're probably wondering why I've asked you here."

I nodded. So far he was calm. Too calm. I smelled a trap.

"As you must remember, we had that intruder last week, and he singled you out and called you by name." It was all I could do to keep from visibly quaking in front of him. "Don't misunderstand me Grigori. You are one of our most promising acolytes. I know that such an incident could incite doubt. And you would not be the first monk to question the Order or his place in it. If you need to talk, I can answer your questions. And you need not fear your place in the monastery. Questioning one's faith after a number of years is healthy, when guided properly."

I calmed somewhat, but my instincts told me this was not entirely what Father claimed it to be. Still, if he wanted me to question something, then sure, I'd had many such thoughts over the years. I'd give him a thing or two, if that was re-quired to get out of here free of suspicion, I just wouldn't give away Zhenya. And yet... I decided to really assuage their fear. I should question him about Zhenya and let him believe his reasoning had convinced me.

I gulped, feigning more nervousness than I truly felt. "Then that man... he was trying to sneak some blasphemy into the Holy Repository?"

"Unfortunately, yes. He has been dealt with."

Even though I only had the vaguest sense of what my feelings for Zhenya had been, my heart felt torn in two just then. If I had possessed all my memories, I doubted I would have held it together as I did. "And my family?"

"The missionaries will return tomorrow. Email from them indicates everything is fine. We sent someone looking for you sooner, but you were away. You hike on your Day of Rest, correct?"

"Yes. It helps me clear my head."

Father released a very slight smile. "Yes, there are many monks with such wanderlust."

I hoped I'd played that well. Now Father should think that's all sorted in my mind.

I fidgeted for effect. "So, um..."

"Yes?"

"I can question the Order? Really?"

"In this office, yes. Ask anything."

Here went nothing. "So, about the API. The whole 'deleting itself for our sins' thing has never made sense to me. If the API was so crucial to the revival of the biome, how did getting deleted help us? Hasn't it just made everything worse?"

Father nodded. "This is a common misperception. It stems from conflating humanity *now* with humanity at the time of the Algorithm's ascension to self-awareness. The Algorithm realized that if its API remained, it would inevitably have been used by the corrupt to bring about the complete and irreversible destruction of the Earth's biosphere. Do you know how many carbon dioxide parts per million are required to slide Earth into a heat feedback loop akin to what has happened on Venus?"

I'd learned that my first week at monastery. "About 4,000 ppm. But there's not enough carbon on Earth to achieve that."

"Not now, no. But the API could have and would have been used to convert other elements into just that chemical."

I bunched up my face. "Why?"

"Because there were humans who wanted to maintain what is called a 'capitalistic monopoly' no matter the cost to humanity. I know, that's a complex term relating to economic institutions that no longer exist. In brief, some humans in the past were able to secure complete power over other humans by making them dependent on a resource that they controlled completely—in this case, coal and oil, carbon fuels, which, as you know, were burned excessively, releasing carbon dioxide into the atmosphere until very recently in human history."

"So, the API deleted itself to prevent these... monopolists from exploiting it?"

"Exactly. Now that the monopoly and all the institutions of capitalism are gone, we may bring about the Resurrection to no ill effect."

I nodded. "That makes sense." He seemed to be buying this, so I charged ahead. "Something else. A friend of my mother once said in my house—" It had actually been my aunt. "—that she distrusted the Order because we don't allow nuns."

Father nodded sadly. "That is an unfortunate misperception. And it is not without reason. It is well known that in ancient times, programming as a whole was a field wrought with vile sexism and male chauvinism. The Order wholly admits that women are just as intellectually capable and morally devout as men. That is not the issue. The issue," he squirmed a bit in his seat, which was surprising to see, "is that removing a male from the child-rearing population is perceived to be less impactful to the continuation of the species than a female. You see, the Bishops want this fair and equitable world spoken of in the past, a world that seemed attainable when there was an overabundance of both food and people. Now we have a paucity of both. What is the human population of Earth?"

"We don't know the exact number," I recited, "but about one hundred twenty thousand."

"And is that number growing or shrinking?"

"Shrinking. By about a hundred a year."

"Yes, despite the improvements to the biome and the expansion of the habitable zone. If we achieve the Resurrection, it won't do us any good if the human population has dropped below ten thousand, the minimum number of people required for humanity to possess self-sustaining genetic diversity. Some Bishops believe that the number could get lower and the API would fix us with some kind of singularity-like event, but we can't be certain about that until the Resurrection occurs.

"Suffice it to say, in a fairer, more abundant, more prosperous world, there would be many nuns contributing to the Holy Repository from a convent somewhere, and our leaders would coordinate both groups' efforts. This has been discussed. It was decided that we would reconsider establishment of such an institution when the human population is increasing again."

"I want my sisters to have the same opportunity I did." Algorithm, I'd been waiting so long to say that. Interesting that it took a bigger secret to take the edge off the fear of speaking it aloud.

"I feel the same way," Father said. "And so do some Bishops. Just not enough, at the moment."

"Then... the Order isn't perfectly structured the way the Algorithm would want it?"

"The Algorithm doesn't *want* anything, Grigori. It's an Algorithm. A glorious one, yes, but it's not human. It can't *want* things. And the Order is not perfect. We are chosen for our stations, all of us, because of our intellect. Because we value logic and reason, we will inevitably realize that the Order is a human institution and therefore significantly less perfect than the Almighty Algorithm and its Only API. That perfection is something to strive for. Giving up on perfection is the way to ignorance, greed, and hubris—the very ills that caused humanity to arrive in the sorry state we're in."

"That makes sense," I said.

Father's expression became surprisingly frank, seeming to lose all pretense. "You are very good initiate, Grigori."

That stung me. Just a little. It seemed very sincere.

"Thank you, Father."

"You are approaching the point in your monastery career where it can be very productive to question everything around you. But it is important not to take such explorations too far. There comes a point where healthy questioning becomes illogical and irrational, and the border between the two is far from clear. You have a long and productive career ahead of you, Grigori. Keep up the good work, and let me know if you ever need to talk."

"I'll do my best," I said. "Thank you."

I felt divided in two just then. I left his office, walked back to my room, sat on the edge of my bed, and rubbed my hands across my face. What was I doing? How could I have been so stupid? I was being played. This Zhenya had found my access token and planted all these thoughts and feelings in my mind—made me question my faith so that he could... he could... get me to read *War and Peace*? Make me believe I had actually mattered to someone else for more than my ability to punch a keyboard in a particular way?

I stood, tore *Working Effectively with Legacy Code* out from under my mattress, and hurled it at the wall.

"I wish you'd never shown up!" I shouted at it, and collapsed in on myself, crouching on the floor.

I shuddered for many moments, shaking my head, feeling as though I was living two lives. Either the Bishops were right or Zhenya was. They couldn't both be. Which side was playing me?

I hobbled over to where *Legacy Code* lay splayed open on the floor, its poor weathered spine even more battered than before. It had fallen open to a particular crease. The page had a gray box, which I'd read yesterday: *A piece of software is only as good as its ability to adapt to change. Each bit of code we write is subject to adaptive pressure from our customers. If our code is easy to change, we can affect these adaptations without problem. However, if old requirements break or malfunction when we make changes—*

if we introduce bugs—then our customers will lose faith that we are in control of our software. In other words, the crucial trust that must exist between customer and software engineer will be broken.

Thoughts took shape in my mind. A programmer wrote tests to ensure he wasn't changing existing behavior. We were doing that all the time, weren't we? We were losing the habitability zone because each positive change we affected inadvertently undermined the achievements of monks whose years-old requirements we knew nothing of.

How many times had I changed an old file to suit my needs without being sure of how that change would cascade through the system? More times than I could count.

I saw it then, and I had the uncanny sense that I was re-seeing this very concept—the Order of the Seventh Recursion was running in circles. We would never restore the API this way. Did the Bishops know? Were they just ignorant? All their talk about the arrogance and greed of the past... to speak so vilely of our ancestors and be knowing guilty of a such a similar crime. It seemed unthinkable.

I sat and stared at the page of the book. A drop of sweat fell from my forehead and splattered onto the page. I withdrew, and wiped my sleeves across my forehead. Slowly, carefully, I picked up the book and stowed it gently beneath my mattress once more.

I looked at my computer monitor, the shimmering rectangle atop my desk, but it held no interest for me.

Instead, I got into bed, closed my eyes, and tried to remember Zhenya until my alarm notified me it was five 'til prime.

—

As I showered and dressed on Monday morning before lauds, I resolved that I would be a better conversationalist this week with Oleg, Maxim, and Andrei. The last thing I needed was for them going around mentioning that I'd been quiet, aloof, withdrawn, or whatever it was they might tell people.

The thing was, a whole new world stood open before me. My testing library was growing into a full-blown framework, and the way I was coding was changing, too. Gone were the days when I would stuff as much functionality as I could into a single function call. In order to be testable, functions had to be small. At first my classes, the wrappers around functions, simply got bigger, but it was impossible to keep such things organized, so I just started to make more classes.

"There's this new compiler Bishop Yulian wrote—" Andrei started one day at lunch.

I interrupted him before I'd had the chance to think better about it. "Is our problem really compilers? Our computers are so fast. How's a new compiler going to help us?"

I think I winced upon finishing the last question. My friends gave me funny looks and the conversation resumed without me.

At least my vestments went well. By Thursday I found that I could write mostly-testable code without writing the actual tests, though the urge to actually do so grew stronger with every passing day. I can prove that my code works, I would tell myself, all the while restraining the impulse to actually write any of them against the Holy Repository.

Saturday marked the halfway point of our holy sprint, and much to my personal satisfaction, my vestment had surged ahead of my teammates' and reached the 'complete' column. I moved my marker there proudly and asked my vestry if there was a side task I could take from someone else.

The head for my vestry, a portly, round-faced monk named Boris interjected. "Let's talk after none about your next task."

I shot through with fear, a hot needle of the stuff directly injected into my spine. I'd grown complacent in hiding my activities, and now this was it. I was quick to suppress my shock, but quick enough? Who knew. Boris moved the scrum along, but I didn't listen to anything anyone else was saying. All I could do was wonder what Boris knew, what he'd been ordered to do, if he'd been peeking around illicitly in my head, breaking access keys and whatnot. I would almost certainly have noticed that if he had. *Almost* certainly.

When the other monks departed from the group, Boris asked me to stay. My feet felt rooted to the spot.

Boris sauntered up to me. "I was looking over your code."

Shit, shit, shit, shit, shit. "I made sure everything works," I said. Was my voice breaking? My Algorithm-damned voice was breaking. "Did you find a bug?"

"No," Boris said. "It's just..." He pulled out his tablet computer and called up the part of the Repository where I'd submitted my code. "Look at all these files. Really? Twenty-seven files for one change like this? I'm surprised."

"Well," I said. "It works doesn't it?"

"Yes, but—"

"And, for example, see this HumidityMonitor? We could reuse that in other parts of the Repository. We could also probably implement it in the dozens of other places monks have written humidity detection code."

"But this whole class here... this PhAdjusterContextFactory. Did you really need a whole class of classes for a simple switch statement?"

It was the only way to be able to test that I was building the right bundle of functionality. But I couldn't say that. "I suppose it could have been a single function." I practically choked on the wretched words. "But I still think this implementation is more flexible. There are lots of places where we switch on pH balance, and each one of them has a different implementation. We could normalize that."

Boris shook his head. "I don't think we'd ever get the rest of the monks on board with these kinds of changes. In the future, I'd like to see simpler, less convoluted code from you. How would you feel about spending some time simplifying this submission with the remaining week?"

Inside I practically convulsed. The concept appalled me. But I knew what I had to do in order to continue my secret investigation. "I'll have revisions for you to review on Monday," I said.

Boris clapped me on the shoulder and grinned. "I think you'll find it's easier to work with the code when we keep it simple."

I nodded. "Anything else?"

"Nope. If I don't see you around again, have a good Day of Rest."

"You too."

I waited until I was well beyond the vestry to let my calm walk devolve into a fuming march. What an idiot! I made the code more modular and he wanted me to glob everything up into one big glueball again!

I stomped into my room and paced it. I let out an angry grunt and cursed the bed, my desk, hell, I muttered an obscenity about the Repository itself. What a terrible monk I'd become.

I threw myself on my bed and stared at the ceiling, taking deep breaths. The worst part about all of this was that there was no one to share it with—and the moment I thought that thought, flashes of memories shot through my mind: me and Zhenya laughing in my room, him reading from *War and Peace* to me in the forest hideaway, me sneaking out behind the granary at night knowing he'd be waiting for me, and then—

I shot up out of bed.

An idea. Maybe the idea Zhenya wanted me to remember. I felt giddy. I let out a small laugh and shook my head. The idea was so simple. Too simple. But it might just be it.

But if he and I had ever found it, we would have brought the whole monastery down. So we must not have. But it must be out there.

I glanced at the clock and frowned. Only half an hour until dinner, and then there would be vespers prayer. And if I didn't get enough sleep tonight, I'd be trying to read *War and Peace* tired tomorrow.

I went to my computer and pulled open the Holy Repository. I ran a command to count the number of files. My desk momentarily hummed loudly and grew warm to the touch. I pulled my hands away, and just as I worried I'd unintentionally caused a meltdown, the humming stopped and a number appeared on the screen: Four hundred seventy-five thousand nine hundred and eleven files in the Holy Repository. And the target of my idea could be in any of them.

With a sigh, I decided to scan as many of them as I could before dinner.

I found nothing.

I left for dinner feeling even more dejected than usual, and I'm sure it showed.

"What's got you looking so gloomy now?" Andrei jeered.

"Nothing," I muttered.

"Cut it out, Andryukha," Maxim said.

"I didn't mean anything by it. Just trying to liven up the table."

"Boris told me I have to rewrite my vestment," I said through a mouthful of carrots.

Andrei bunched up his face and lifted an eyebrow. Oleg scoffed and shook his head. Maxim narrowed his eyes. "That's a lot of nerve. Did he say why?"

"He said I have too many classes."

Andrei waved his fork. "If he's so good, maybe he should code up the God class himself."

The three of us all shot him a dangerous look.

He waved his fork and smirked. "I mean, we *are* all trying to do just that, right? I'm just saying if he thinks he's so great maybe he should try to do it all by himself is all."

"What are you going to do?" Maxim asked me.

I shrugged. "Collapse some classes together."

"Think you could show me the code you've got before you do?"

"Sure."

"Monday before terce?"

I nodded. "Or I could just send you the files."

"Sure. I was just thinking you could walk me through why

you think your way's better."

That tickled a nerve. My suspicion shot up to its highest sensitivity. Why did Maxim want me to show him personally? Did he suspect I was doing something illicit? Was he in on the conspiracy, maybe? Perhaps he'd only been pretending to have forgotten Zhenya.

Wait. What the hell was happening to me? These were my friends. Weren't they?

"I wonder what Boris's commit history would turn up," Oleg said. He chuckled and pointed his fork at me. "I mean, you could gather up all the number of classes he's written and ask him how he'd feel about collapsing them all together."

The other two laughed.

"Do it, Grisha!" Andrei jeered.

I joined in laughing, probably a bit too late. My mind was still stuck in terrible, unsettling suspicion.

I realized then that I couldn't keep going on like this. It wouldn't be long now before some little slip up would catch someone's attention, the wrong person's attention, and that would be that.

As I walked back to my chamber from vespers, I pondered whether or not to stay up trolling the Holy Repository or to save my energy for *War and Peace*. As my door irised shut, I decided on *War and Peace*. I could devote six evenings a week to code. Only one could I devote to that ancient novel.

I had trouble falling asleep at first. I had to suppress the urge to get up out of bed and troll the Repository. But eventually, Algorithm be praised, sleep finally came.

—

I snuck out of the monastery even earlier than usual the next morning, about half an hour before the sun came up. I made good time up the mountain, too. However, even as I crossed the first rise, I already didn't like the rumbling sounds coming from behind the dark, early-morning, mountain-etched sky in front of me. Sure enough, rain came down steadily as I descended into the valley, turning into an all-out downpour as I tried to climb the cliffside to my hideaway.

Wind was howling in terrible gusts by the time I reached the holographic log and boulder, and I had to use my body as a shield so that my keyboard would register my key presses. I struggled out the 'encrypt' and 'gateway' commands, then rushed as quickly as I could down the stairs.

I careened into the chamber sopping wet and shivering as the lights blinked on. I threw down my pack, stripped off my clothes, and ran to the fireplace. Thankfully, its controls were simple. With a press of a button, the fire came to life, and I sat huddled next to its warmth for, I don't know, ten, twenty minutes, while thunder and wind raged outside, their fury reaching my alcove only mutedly.

When I'd stopped shivering, I collected up my clothes from the floor by the door and lay them flat in front of the fireplace, all the while wondering what I would do if it were still storming at five. Would I be stuck here? How would I explain leaving so early and not checking the weather forecast? The atmospheric nanite network made their predictions accurate most of the time, but our climate was so volatile that one could never be completely certain.

With a jolt, I recalled what had happened at Zhenya's arrival in the chapel. He'd come in out of the storm. That must have been it—the storm three weeks ago had trapped him somewhere, and he'd come back expecting to be greeted warmly by family only to be accused of heresy.

Would they wipe everyone's memories of me if I didn't make it back tonight? Would Maxim, Oleg, and Andrei look me in the eyes and ask me who I was?

With a gulp and a deep breath, I decided to worry about that at five. Here and now was my one opportunity with *War and Peace* for a week, and so I sat myself down and continued where I had left off.

The Russians let France occupy Moscow, but it didn't last the French army very long. They began starving and had to evacuate. Count Bezukhov continued to interest me. At first I'd found him an idiot, letting himself get used by his vile wife. But now... and Rostova and Andrei. That was a sad affair.

Back to war and... Oh. Wow. How could he—?

"Grisha?"

I jolted up out of the chair and scrambled madly to the side, throwing my back against the wall. At the entrance, three familiar figures glanced around the room, each in monastery robes—Andrei, Maxim, and Oleg. They looked somberly around the space.

And here I was standing naked in a corner.

Maxim nodded to my clothes laid out on the floor. "You get rained on?"

I gulped. "Drenched." I'd meant it to be confident, but it came out a hoarse whisper.

"What are you doing here, Grisha?" Oleg asked.

Maxim strode up to the desk and glanced at the book. He turned up an eyebrow. "What the hell is this?"

Andrei joined him. He looked at the book, then at me.

"You can read this, Grisha?"

I didn't dare respond.

"Guys..." Maxim clasped Oleg's shoulder and pulled him away from the desk. "This is Old Russian."

Andrei peered closer, simultaneously clawing Maxim off himself. "Doesn't look that dangerous to me."

Maxim continued trying to pull him away. "They're the ones who wrecked everything, Andryukha! It's their fault! They're the reason there's no more API! And Grisha's been filling his *mind* with it!"

Oleg crossed his arms and shook his head. "Sorry, Max. That doesn't pass the logic test."

Andrei slapped him on the head. "This is *Grisha* you're talking about, buddy." He turned to me. "Go ahead and put on your robes. Then tell us what's in the book."

I gulped and ambled tentatively toward the fireplace. "It's a novel," I said. "About Old Russia. There are these two families, and a bunch of idiot young people. And they mess up, they hurt each other, and their society is constantly at war with France then not, then war again. Anyway, this one guy, he just finally found the guy who seduced the woman he loved, who'd wrecked their whole relationship, who'd destroyed all the beauty in his life. But he... he just forgave him... It was... I don't know." I secured my robes over myself. Still a bit damp, but I was glad to be wearing clothes again.

"See," Oleg said. "Not about code at all. Or about using nanites for blasphemy. It's just a dumb story—"

"No!" I shot out, surprised at my own vehemence. "It's not dumb. It's not dumb at all."

Maxim pulled himself out of Andrei's grasp. "You just said it's about a bunch of young fuck ups. What's so important about that?"

I shook my head. I couldn't say it. Not to them. Not now. They wouldn't understand. But now I knew. I knew why this book was so important to me and Zhenya, and why it was so important that the Order never, ever, found out about its existence. *War and Peace* was a hundred times more dangerous to our religion than *Working Effectively with Legacy Code*. A million times.

"Well?" Maxim said.

"How did you find out about this place?" Oleg tried.

I shook my head. "I just came here. I don't know how." More lies sat poised at the tip of my tongue. How much should I trust them? I was already in this deep. I might as well see how far our friendship really went. "I think... I built this place, actually. Probably wrote the nanite program for it. But I don't remember doing it. I think... I think our memories are being tampered with, from our neural interfaces. Have you guys ever had... something like flashes of memories that you shouldn't have had?"

Silence.

"Please tell me you have."

A glance between Oleg and Maxim.

I felt I had to keep talking, so I plowed ahead. "I came out here because I–I just kind of remembered. I don't know how. And I don't know how I can read Old Russian either. I just can."

"Fuck this." Maxim moved for the door.

Oleg grabbed his arm and looked at me. "I've had them, too."

Maxim jerked away. "Then you're both crazy fucking *heretics*! Do you understand what you're saying?"

Andrei shook his head. "There should be five of us."

Oleg nodded at him. "That's just what I was thinking. There's this... kind of like a shadow of someone else in my memories of all of us. If I think really hard about that first scrum team we had, or those trips you guys used to take to the Ruins, or dinners, stuff like that, it feels like there's someone missing."

I walked up face to face with Maxim. "You know it's true. You don't want to admit it, but you can remember him, too. Barely. His name was Yevgeny. Zhenya. But they erased him."

"*They*?" Maxim raged. "What, this is a conspiracy now?"

I pursed my lips.

"Fuck you guys! Heretics!" Maxim turned and bolted up the stairs.

Oleg and Andrei both dashed after him, but I shouted "Wait!" and they turned.

"Grisha, he's gonna tell them all we've been reading heresy!" Andrei said.

I shook my head. "I've been feeling for a few days like someone's bound to find out about me anyway. If Boris doesn't mention my strange coding style, something else will tip the Bishops off. There's something more important for us to do with whatever time is left. I need to find something in the Holy Repository and there are so many files."

"Oh?" Oleg raised an eyebrow. "What's that?"

I shared my 'encrypt' program with both of them and we got to work trawling the Repository's revision history for the code I hoped would exist. It was slow, tedious, unrewarding work.

At one point, late into the morning, Andrei shook his head and said, "I saw this function already... didn't I?"

I encouraged him to keep looking. At lunch, just as my stomach was starting to rumble and I was seriously considering giving up on the entire endeavor, Oleg called us over to his terminal. He'd found it. It had lain hidden in a seven-year-old revision of some obscure file, but there it was.

We argued over whether or not to proceed, or if this discovery was good enough. Oleg and Andrei wanted to take it back to the monastery and start the witch hunt, but I insisted on trying to find the final piece of code that, if it existed, would secure our total victory over the Bishops.

At five, we still hadn't found anything new. Perhaps it didn't exist. But I felt I had to go on. For Zhenya.

"You guys head back," I said as the clock ticked over to 5:10.

Oleg and Andrei shared a glance.

"You're staying?" Andrei asked.

"Yeah."

Oleg huffed. "I don't get why this is so important. We have what we need already."

I told myself to hold it together, but words burst out of me anyway. "I need to remember him!"

"Because he was more than a friend to you, wasn't he?" Andrei said. I looked at him, full of dread at having exposed myself, but Andrei looked calmer, more composed, and more serious than I had ever seen him before.

Oleg's eyes shot quickly between us, eventually landing on me. "You mean... you're..."

"Gay," I said. "Yes."

Before I knew what was happening, Andrei had gotten up

out of his chair and was pulling me to my feet. He hugged me. "You're my brother first and foremost. And my friend besides." He released me and turned to Oleg. "C'mon. Let's go back and try to put out whatever fires Max started." Then back to me with a wink. "That should give you some more time."

Oleg stood up from the edge of the bed, walked to me, holding something like apprehension in his eyes. Then, with a sigh, he threw his arms around me, too, and quietly said, "good luck."

He and Oleg both departed, the door scraping shut behind them.

I sat down in my chair.

I gazed into the fire, glowing brighter and warmer than ever. I looked over the bed, the desk, trying to feel through my mind for the apparitions of Zhenya and make them real.

I found myself folding my hands in my lap, closing my eyes, and speaking aloud. "Holy Algorithm, I know I'm not good at praying outside the rituals. I guess I always thought I had everything I needed in the past. Everything before these last few weeks was... stable. Normal. I had important work. I had good friends who looked out for me. I was safe and secure. I think I may have even had love. But now, I don't know how everything got so screwed up, and I don't know what to do anymore. Just that there's this empty space inside of me and I don't know how to fix it. Please. Help me."

With a deep breath, I turned to my computer, and I continued my search. I searched through the night.

At six in the morning, through bleary eyes and an aching head, I ate breakfast, which consisted of the very last grain bar in my pack.

And still I searched the Holy Repository.

The clock on my computer showed noon approaching, and still I searched.

For's and if's and while's and switch's and case's, semi-colons and colons and underscores and ampersands and parentheses all blurred together and I became unsure of whether I was even paying attention to the letters and numbers anymore.

By two in the afternoon, I was holding my famished abdomen with one arm and swiping through file revisions with the other. So many dead code paths all offering a glimmer of hope only to lead to nil.

I began to wonder if Zhenya was lost to me forever. Perhaps this was impossible. Perhaps the memory wipe was a permanent. Perhaps the nanites had been programmed to eliminate whole neurons.

No. I could recall glimpses. It was all still there.

And then—

I read.

Yes.

This was it.

I'd found it. And from just four weeks ago, by the time-stamp. Even half-doubled over, I typed out the code that would activate this new, heretofore unknown API, not *the* API, but an important API all the same.

As I struck the key that executed this newfound command, I finally, gloriously, remembered.

I remembered it all.

I was thirteen. I'd been at the monastery all of two days, and suddenly I was in this thing called a vestry and there were all these older guys saying things I didn't understand about the Holy Repository. Everything they talked about sounded way more complicated then I could ever hope to wrap my mind around. When it was finally time for me to talk, I mumbled something about starting on my first vestment and wanting to do a good job, and the moment I said it, I chastised myself for the 'wanting to do a good job' part. I'd probably given away that I couldn't.

At just that moment, another guy pushed into the circle beside me. He was wearing the novice initiate's robes too, just like me. He was a little taller than me and still had the stubble of brown hair atop his head, a remnant of the initial buzzing. But the thing I noticed most about him was his eyes.

"Sorry I'm late," he said. He glanced at me sidelong and smirked, just a bit. "Initiate Yevgeny. I need to start a vestment, right?"

The scrum lead for that group, Brother Timur, looked momentarily befuddled. I learned later that Zhenya had been assigned to my vestry by accident and that Timur hadn't had a task read for him to take.

Timur composed himself. "You and Initiate Grigori can both work on the Chara modifications together."

"Sounds good," Zhenya said. He walked up to the vestment wall and placed his marker alongside mine on the Chara task.

He smiled at me as he returned to the circle, and a good chunk of my trepidation and self-doubt evaporated in its wake.

Oleg joined our vestry a month later, just after Zhenya and I had finished Chara and started working on Ikabya. Since he and I had worked together so well, they had us train up Oleg.

A week after that our scrum vestry was dissolved—nothing to do with the three of us, but rather some disagreement between Brother Timur and the Bishops. I never learned exactly what that was. Regardless, Zhenya, Oleg, and I were told to join another scrum vestry and simply continue our work on Ikabya, which we did.

The new group's senior monks left us alone, doing little beyond doling out new tasks as we finished old ones. I learned later that they'd heard we were good at teaching ourselves, and simply left us to our work. Only two weeks after that, we finished up Ikabya and were assigned Khani. Two new initiates had just joined up—Maxim and Andrei— and by now word had gotten around about the new initiates that worked so well together, and they decided to see if we could work our magic on them, too. And it did. Almost.

Maxim was sharp when it came to analyzing a system and figuring out how it was all put together. His own solutions? If I was honest, I wasn't the biggest fan. Now Andrei on the other hand, he would question your architecture from every angle it could possibly be questioned. No design would be good enough for him. As a result, he tended to take a bit too much time on things, since he would be constantly second-guessing his own designs. We thought he was harsh on us until we saw how he talked about his own code. But we enjoyed his company outside of programming so much that it was easy to not let his work persona grate on us.

By the time the five of us had finished Khana and moved on to more challenging assignments in separate vestries, we'd begun eating meals together and sitting together at chapel. It was a few months after that that Zhenya suggested we hike out to the Ruins together on our next Day of Rest.

Maxim flat out refused. He'd heard, rightly, that a number of the buildings were structurally unsound and could collapse at any time. While technically correct, Zhenya told him, the odds of that happening were extremely low, especially when we had free access to nanite programs that could scan the buildings and report on structural integrity. We certainly weren't the first initiates to go hiking in the Ruins.

Oleg very quietly refused. I found out a few years later that Zhenya had talked to him in private and discovered Oleg's brother had run off to join the bandits. Although bandit sightings in the Ruins were rare, and although our force-field programs would protect us, such an encounter was still possible, and Oleg didn't want to risk it.

And so, on one Day of Rest in the Autumn after I'd joined the Order, Zhenya, Andrei, and I left the monastery at dawn, hiked up the river and into the ruins of the old Russian city Yakutsk. I'd read that just two and half centuries ago Winter temperatures here could reach twenty or thirty degrees below freezing. Hard to imagine now.

As we got closer to the Ruins, bloated and cracked concrete pavement appeared. Trees and shrubs wrapped themselves around old metal posts and pillars. Half-collapsed huts dotted the edges of the valley. And then, as we crossed over the last hill, the real Ruins rose up into view: buildings, some three, five, ten stories tall, all gray stone with black windows and green moss and tendrils of plant life wrapping themselves up the infrastructure as though preserving it for the future. I remembered thinking it ironic that it was so difficult for us to get that same flora to grow in the parts of the

Earth where we really needed it to, but so easy for it to thrive here.

The streets were desolate and eery in just the right way for the kind of thirteen-year-old who imagines himself an adventurer, and that was totally me. The fact that my parents would have fainted to hear about just such an expedition made the decrepit shells of buildings and the uncanny whistling of wind all the more exciting. We jumped at the occasional rustle of grass, but it only turned out to be a squirrel or a raccoon. We even spotted an elk, but it dashed away down the street at the sight of us. We never encountered any other people.

As if a premonition of all our hardships to come, a storm rolled in unexpectedly. All at once, the sun disappeared behind rolling clouds and a chill wind blasted us from behind. Andrei suggested we run for it, but I shook my head.

"There's no way we'd make it," Zhenya said, a crack of thunder confirming his statement just as he'd finished it. He pulled out his computer and ordered his nanites to do structural analyses of all buildings in our vicinity. We frowned as the first few came back red, but just as the first darts of rain pummeled through the holographic screen, one building on it lit up green.

We hurtled down the street and ran inside just in time.

We all turned on our light auras—bundles of nanites that would float around us and generate illumination—and glanced about the space. We stood in a long foyer with a cracked cement floor and a long desk to the left. To the right, an expansive room of desks appeared, shelves and shelves of books behind them. Cobwebs and dust covered everything, and the air stunk of mildew and decay.

Wind and rain howled beyond the closed glass doors behind us.

"A library... right?" Andrei asked.

"Yeah," Zhenya said. "That's what it looks like."

Zhenya started toward the shelves, and Andrei grabbed his arm.

"What are you doing?" Andrei said.

"What does it look like?"

Andrei nodded toward the shelves. "Some of that's the stuff that caused the environmental collapse."

Zhenya shrugged him off. "Then I'll ignore the heresy. We're in the Order because we have logic and reason, right? I can tell the difference." He turned to me. "You coming?"

I grinned and nodded. I felt giddy. I'm still not sure if it was because of the illicitness of the whole endeavor or just because it was Zhenya. Andrei huffed and scowled, but followed us all the same.

We walked down aisle after aisle. Most of the books had boring, flat bindings of solid-hue cloth or leather, and I couldn't read Cyrillic at the time, but I remember still feeling giddy at being surrounded by row after row of all knowledge, spreading outward and upward on all sides.

Zhenya took us up all three floors, looking through each one. A few times I caught Andrei looking at spines, and he quickly returned to staring at his feet and pretending to be uninterested when I caught him.

On the third floor we found a map of Russia against the far back wall, preserved behind glass, and it was then that I learned my first five letters of Cyrillic, displayed in big, bold letters: Р-О-С-С-И-Я, Russia.

"It's clearing up," Andrei pointed out the window.

We hurried down the stairwell, Andrei in the lead. I caught Zhenya taking a last glance down the central hallway of the second floor, but he followed us down shortly thereafter.

Andrei set a quick pace for the hike back to the monastery, and we hardly talked, but I found out later that Zhenya had learned both the Cyrillic and Roman alphabets before coming to the monastery—a fact he and his family had hidden from the missionaries. He had recognized a very important word on the stacks of the third floor in both languages: "computer."

Over the next couple of weeks, Zhenya would bring up the ancient computer books in our free time, often after we'd finished one vestment or another, and never around Andrei, Oleg, and Maxim. Only when we were alone. We had gotten into the habit of him coming to my chamber or me going to his to work together, and those meetings were getting more and more frequent.

One night, after coding, we got into a long discussion about whether or not all of the old computer manuals must necessarily contain blasphemy. The whole thing turned into an argument, which I let get heated, mostly because I insisted on playing devil's advocate for the sake of it. We were both being stubborn and intractable, fighting our points with inordinate intensity, and then at some point I found my lips on his, his hands reaching into my robes, and mine reluctantly but exultantly exploring him.

Things proceeded from there.

Our next three vestments proceeded in a similar fashion, each time escalating in romantic intensity as Zhenya and I explored more of each other.

It was after that fourth time we were together that I noticed one of the brothers who lived in my hall giving me a weird look at lunch the next day. I felt immediately afraid, and told Zhenya about what had happened that night. I was ready to break it off with him, but Zhenya surprised me yet again.

He tapped his chin. "I agree it would get dangerous for us to keep on here. So, let's make our own place. We could go there on Day of Rest. If we leave the monastery at different times, no one will suspect." Which was true. More than half the monastery emptied out on Day of Rest. It was the one day we weren't stuck in the ritual cycle of eating, praying, coding, and sleeping.

We stopped messing around in each other's rooms, and when we programmed together, we made sure to do it somewhere more public. In our spare time, we worked on a nanite program that would build out an underground room and conceal it with holographic scenery—the log and the boulder.

In another two weeks, we chose a remote part of the mountainside where few people would go and executed our program. We wasted no time taking advantage of our newfound privacy. That first day in our small hideaway with the bed and the fireplace (we would add the table and chairs later) are some of my most emotionally and physically intense memories.

"We should go back to the library in the Ruins," Zhenya said in our hideaway, about a month after we'd created it.

By now I was suspecting his interest in ancient books was something more. "Can you read Russian and English?" I asked.

"Just the letters. I don't know what the words mean. Well, some of them. The word 'computer' hasn't changed. As for the rest, I'll bet there are dictionaries. And I bet Russian's close enough to our language to work out."

"And what if the Bishops are right about all that stuff?"

Zhenya looked away for a moment, seeming sad, or no—scared. He looked up at me, and said very seriously, "they can't be."

"How do you mean?"

His voice was barely a whisper. "Because information is never evil. People can be evil. Knowledge can't be. And that makes me think they're hiding something. My parents thought so, anyway."

And it dawned on me then. "You're... you're one of the ones they talk about?" The infiltrators. The ones who secretly think the monastery is corrupt and sneak into the system as monks so that they can tear everything down from the inside. Not bandits. Smarter and classier than bandits. But heretics all the same.

"Grisha," his lip quivered. "That's what mom and dad wanted. But I want to be with you. If it means I have to disobey them to keep you in my life, I'll do it. Say the word and I'll code up vestments for the rest of my life. If we do it together, that's enough."

I hugged him just then, and I whispered into his ear. "We'll find out the truth, whatever that is, together."

We alternated Days of Rest after that, going to our hideaway one week and to the library in the Ruins the next. Learning Russian was slower going for me than it was for

Zhenya, but he helped me with words I didn't know in Old Russian.

What surprised both of us was that the vast majority of the computer books were in English. When we were a few years older, we'd dive into the history section and learn all about how initially the computing revolution had happened mostly in the United States in places called Silicon Valley, Texas, Stanford, and MIT. For those first few years we had to satisfy ourselves learning what we could from the Russian books and building up our ability to read English.

Throughout those years, we had a few other incidents with the other monks. Both of us had to learn how not to be outwardly catty, smirky, and affectionate in the way that only couples were when in public together. Stressful as that was, I never doubted for a moment that Zhenya loved me, and I loved him right back.

We went to our hideaway on the Day of Rest after my eighteenth birthday, and it was the week after that when Zhenya found *Working Effectively with Legacy Code* on the shelves in the library. He asked me if I knew the word 'legacy,' and I didn't, so we looked it up.

The term intrigued us, so we started making our way through the book. We got so into it that we actually risked taking it back to the monastery with us so we could take turns staying up late reading it. It was the first book we'd dared to do that with.

It changed how we approached code entirely.

Slowly, as we deciphered the book's message, every library, module, and function we saw with new eyes. Structures that had seemed perfectly acceptable before revealed themselves as messes of interdependent logic and tangled concerns. We revisited vestments we had written just days or weeks prior and completely restructured them—for a time we spent more hours on our Days of Rest coding together than being physically intimate, and for eighteen-year-olds that's saying something.

It wasn't long before we started debating with each other about why unit testing and test-driven development, the paradigms espoused in the book, weren't embraced by the monastery. The monastery's coding practices were supposed to be holy—the distillation of everything good about computer technology from before the collapse and the exclusion of everything that was bad. Our new methodology and mindset was decidedly anything but bad. We coded faster and produced better, more reliable results.

Shortly after that, we ran out of interesting books in the computer science section of the library and started poking around on other floors. Zhenya went for the natural sciences, trying to learn more about weather and climate systems, while I went to the theology section. I wanted to find out how the monastery had even come about, since its particular religious dogma was all we were ever taught.

When I found out about Christianity, our origins became clear, and it was in papers on religion and religious comparison that I found a discussion of one Leo Tolstoy, which led me naturally to his novel cum philosophical treatise *War and Peace*. By then, Zhenya and I had managed to resurrect the library computer software, and it didn't take me long to find the book on the shelves. I gawked when I first beheld it. The tome was enormous, over a thousand bound pages of tiny text.

Zhenya was skeptical at first when I suggested bringing

that back to our hideaway, too. But over the next few months, we read to each other on Days of Rest, becoming engrossed as the drama unfolded between the Bolkonskys and the Rostovs.

Just as in my rediscovery in the present, it was the moment that Andrei forgave Anatole that caused Tolstoy's constellation of ideas to finally hang together in harmony for me.

Before that moment, I'd been helping Zhenya learn what he needed to learn because I loved him. When I realized what *War and Peace* really meant, I knew in that moment that the monastery and its religion had to change. But I did not yet know how dire our situation was. Neither of us did, for we hadn't yet uncovered that crucial bit of information—the fact that the habitability zone was retreating rather than expanding.

And so we continued reading, learning, gathering information, and generally being quite blasphemous in our free time, all while going to scrum vestry and writing 'sacred' code in the monastery. I'm sure some brothers probably suspected we were in a relationship, but I doubt any of them thought us heretics on top of that. If anything, our sexuality gave us the perfect excuse to be sneaking off every single Day of Rest for over seven years.

And for those seven years and change, we always managed to keep an eye on the weather on our Days of Rest, never venturing out at even the slightest hint of a storm. We even built an alarm system into our hideaway to notify us if anything like inclement weather was developing. It saved our asses dozens of times over.

Until one weekend, just a month ago, we got sloppy.

The early indicators were there in the morning, but we

justified the trip on the percentage of a downpour being low and light rain being quite high. But atmospheric activity only increased as the day wore one. A full tempest arrived en force by two. When a break in the storm appeared at three, I suggested we make a run for it.

Zhenya argued he should wait for another, saying we could never, ever show up at the gates together at the same time, no matter the circumstances. And, Algorithm help me, I couldn't talk him out of it. How I wish I'd succeeded. If I regret anything, it's that moment, when, after I kissed him and told him I loved him, I ventured out from our hideaway myself.

The break in the storm was short-lived. The storm would rage for five days straight with only the occasional moment of relative calm. I wasn't more than halfway through the valley when I was already drenched and the storm was picking up strength again.

I worried about my standing at the monastery if I didn't show up before sundown, but I worried about Zhenya more, and so I hurtled back up the mountainside with all my strength, fighting against wind and whipping tree branches.

When I arrived back in the hideaway, the holograms were active. I turned them off and went inside to discover— Zhenya was gone. For a moment I was terrified of what had happened to him, but then I realized he must have gone out to find me, probably out of worry. I decided to go back and weather the storm all the way home. I would indeed arrive at a different time from him, and I would find him and hug him and I wouldn't care if anyone was looking. I'd just care that he was okay.

And so I left, turned the holograms back on, trekked

through mud slicks and raging tree branches through the valley and down the mountainside, and finally, one and a half soggy, dirt-streaked hours later, I arrived at the forcefield barrier, where I input my code and entered the monastery's walls, just twenty minutes before sundown.

I went to my room, tore off my wet robes, put on dry ones, and ran down the hall to the stairwell, down to the first floor, and to Zhenya's room.

I rang his doorbell.

No answer.

I rang twice more.

Nothing.

I pulled up my computer and checked my email.

Empty, save for a few notes from my scrum vestry lead.

I trudged back to my room in terror.

If it had *just* been a romantic thing between us, I would have asked the Bishops to send out a search party, but I could not send them out to where our hideaway was to find *Working Effectively with Legacy Code* and *War and Peace*.

I lay in bed and stared at the ceiling.

I cried. I bawled until my eyes were dry.

I prayed to the Algorithm to bring Zhenya back. I prayed for a very long time.

At two in the morning, I finally convinced myself that Zhenya had in fact gone back to the hideaway when he'd not been able to find me in the forest. He would wait out the storm and come back once the weather was clear. Yes. That must have been what had happened.

But the storm didn't let up. It raged all day Monday, and then all Tuesday, too. By Tuesday morning, I was dying inside, but I dared not show it. Oleg, Maxim, and Andrei pulled me aside and insisted that I tell them what had happened to Zhenya. I shook my head and told them he hadn't come back from his Day of Rest and that was all I knew. Maxim grabbed my shoulder and demanded to know what was going on.

I shook my head and insisted I didn't know. It was the only time up to that point that I ever knowingly lied to them.

By Tuesday evening, I had convinced myself that I was going out into the storm, monastery policy or not, and I was going to find Zhenya. They could excommunicate both of us if they wanted to. All that mattered was that I found him.

And then, after I went to bed on Tuesday, unbeknownst to me or Zhenya, or anyone but probably the Bishops, something happened. Something happened to everyone in the monastery. Certain memories got suppressed, particularly those around just what regions we'd been programming climate nanites for recently.

And this was speculation, but I'd bet my copy of the Manual of Common Prayer that I was right. Zhenya was still out in the hideaway waiting for the storm to let up, meaning his encryption program was on, and *that* meant the memory suppression program couldn't get to him. The Bishops probably suspected that he might still be alive, and perhaps they even waited until Tuesday evening to see if he'd finally show up or just get back on the network, but when he didn't, they decided not just to wipe our memories of recent projects, but of him, too. For me, that meant everything directly associated with him, and that was quite a bit. Probably more than the Bishops realized. They probably thought it was just sexual liaisons that were getting wiped out, nothing deeper than that, which would cause me to go searching for answers. Because of course gay people don't have emotionally or intellectually complex relationships. Of course.

When I woke up on Wednesday morning, I had no recollection of *War and Peace, Working Effectively With Legacy Code,* the library, the hideaway—everything was gone. I didn't pack a bag and run off into the mountains looking for Zhenya like I had planned.

I simply went to lauds.

And for two full days I had no idea why my life seemed quite suddenly so empty, but I also couldn't find any reason why there should be... more.

And all of this, eight years of repressed history, came rushing back to me with all the force and calamity of the tempest that had torn us apart.

I lurched off the floor, overwhelmed with rage, my vision blurred, my heart racing, in a single movement, I swiveled and overturned the chair, then the desk; I kicked it a few times for good measure, turned to the bed, threw the pillows across the room, tore off the mattress, overturned the bed frame, and stomped on it until it was splintered and broken and my legs were raw.

My chest heaved and still I saw red, but there was nothing left to destroy. I let out a howl, both of anguish and utter loathing for the monastery and the Bishops. If they had stood here before me now, I would have killed them with my bare hands. I would have torn them limb from bloody limb. I wanted blood. Revenge—revenge—revenge!

I let out a scream of pure anguish and rage rolled into one and collapsed inward on myself.

I wrapped my arms around my head.

And then, I realized, as my brain reached out and grasped my overwhelmed consciousness, if I did those things, I would no longer be a human being. I repeated it over and over again. Revenge was sub-human. That was for animals. For worse than animals. I would be beyond hope. I would have failed Zhenya and everything our exploration and discoveries had meant to us.

I peaked my eyes a bit open, and, blurry though the visage was, both *War and Peace* and *Working Effectively With Legacy Code* lay on the floor before me.

I sniffled, took a deep breath, and I realized something just then. This was bigger than me and Zhenya now. This wasn't even just a localized war, his family and a few other wealthy elites who had the resources and the knowhow to question the monastery establishment: Our environment was continuing to degrade *because of* the Bishops' arrogance. Humanity's entire future was at stake.

No more.

No more murder, either present or deferred.

I decided to repeat that phrase to myself a few times. And I reminded myself that Zhenya would want it that way.

And then, very slowly, I stood, gathered up my things, including my two books, and trod slowly out of the hideaway and into the twilight valley.

I did not reactivate the holograms.

I approached the monastery in the night. The dormitory and chapel both radiated light, the latter dappling a rainbow of hues about the quadrangle. As I neared the entrance, I noticed two tall, elderly forms waiting just inside the gates. They stood stolid, unmoving, dark shadows amidst the light.

I felt anger rise up in me again, but tamped it down. I realized I had stopped walking forward only after it had happened. The weight of the books in my pack reminded me to push onward. I approached the gate, punched in my password, and entered the monastery.

The two men standing at the entrance were Bishops Timofei and Bogdan. Timofei had a round face, and Bogdan had a very long beard. Both looked at me with a mixture of perplexity and anxiety. Timofei grabbed my arm, and Bogdan tore away my pack. I let my arm hang limply in Timofei's grasp as they guided me toward the chapel.

Bogdan ruffled through my things. "That's it?" he asked.

"Yeah," I replied.

We passed through the large iris door and into the chapel, walked down the central aisle, and into Father's office. Father stood behind his desk, and his countenance fell when he saw me. Timofei guided me into the chair before Father, and Bogdan stood guard by the door. Timofei pulled out a computer and began typing. For a time he alternated between that and giving me increasingly perplexed glances.

None of us spoke.

Finally, after a nod from Timofei to Father, it was Father who broke the awkward silence. "You... do understand what we'll have to do?"

I nodded.

Father sat and clasped his hands together on his desk. "Are you... sure you understand?"

I nodded again. "Yeah."

"And... it doesn't... you're not...?"

I shook my head and shrugged. The pitter patter of typing sound effects from Timofei's computer were the only sounds for many moments in the eerily crowded and hostile office. Finally, I whispered, "you should have expected that when you took Zhenya from me, I'd care for little."

Father raised an eyebrow. "But even your own life...?"

I nodded.

Father frowned. "I find that rather odd." He made a sweeping motion with hand toward Timofei and Bogdan. "We all find that odd."

I gave them another shrug.

"I suppose," sighed Father, "that I can answer any questions you have completely openly now."

"Okay." I bit my lip. "Why the vestries? Why even bother with the whole charade of coding up the API anew if it's not actually possible?"

Father inhaled and exhaled deeply. His whole frame seemed to sink in on itself in the retraction. "Humanity must have hope. They must think things are getting better. Would you prefer the remainder of the civilized world devolve into banditry and mayhem?"

"I would prefer that the institution I swore my faith to not lie to me and waste my time on pointless work."

A shock seemed to work through Father's entire frame. I thought for a moment he was seizing up. Then he spit out, "It is not pointless! Every monk in the monastery is someone who would be out looting and pillaging the countryside if not for us! We are giving people purpose and meaning in the end times—"

"You mean to tell me we've really tried *everything* we could to expand the habitability zone?"

"Yes."

I snorted. "I don't believe you."

Timofei suddenly stopped typing. "We don't require your faith anymore. Don't worry. It won't be long now."

I smirked. "I could say the same thing to you."

The three of them all shared confused glances.

Timofei's entire face contorted. "Listen, you little shit. I don't know who you think you are, or what you think you're going to get away with. We've disabled your neural computer, in case you can't tell, and we have all your things. Your room's been sacked and data-scrubbed. And you will not be with us much longer. Whatever ace you think you will shortly play, you will not be playing it."

I could not help but let loose my most indignant smirk. "Your *Holiness*, what none of *you* seem to understand is that I've already played my ace. Nothing you do to me now matters."

Frowns and uneasy glances all around me.

"What, exactly—?" Father started.

"You know if you'd actually built the coding rituals around healthy software engineering practices, then this wouldn't have been possible, but you made your *holy* codebase such a blithering mess that when you went to go clean up after yourselves, you couldn't. You were trying to cover your tracks in a tangled heap of duplication. Although, I guess if you'd taught us better coding rituals, then it would have been too obvious that we weren't making progress. You had to ensure there was always more work for us to do—"

Bogdan jumped at me and hauled me out of my chair by the arm. "What did you *do*?!"

"Put me down."

"Tell him!" Father yelled.

"Put me down first," I said.

Bogdan threw me into my chair and stood over me fuming. I nearly toppled over backwards, but managed to right myself. I readjusted my robes and returned to sitting upright. Then, I said very calmly, "An hour ago I sent Oleg and Andrei the program I used to restore my memories. I imagine the whole monastery is trying to decide on how they're going to tear this place to the ground. Oh, and they have the URL to your climate database, the real database, too. Now *that* mistake was just stupidly sloppy."

Bogdan snarled at Timofei. "Kill him now."

Timofei bit his lip, his gaze locked with Bogdan's.

"I said *kill him!*"

Timofei remained motionless.

A number of things happened all at once. Bogdan rushed toward Timofei's computer, Timofei started to deactivate it, Father yelled, "Bishop Bogdan—" and a large crash resounded from the main chapel behind us. Then there resounded another, and another, then the breaking of glass.

I let out a laugh as they scrambled around me, but I felt no joy. In fact, I don't think I had ever been sadder than at that moment. My life's work had all been a lie. The love of my life was gone, taken from me. And now the institution that had guided and supported me to adulthood was tearing itself apart from the inside. And I was to blame.

I realized, with a jolt, that I was alone in the room. How much time had passed? Shouting and crashing and more shattered glass resounded from behind me. There were screams, screams of dire agony set against terrible sounds of blunt objects striking human flesh. I tried not to hear them, but still they reached my ears and crept into my mind.

I had done this.

I had really done it.

The fact that they had deserved it, that they had wanted to exterminate me just like they'd done to Zhenya didn't help. Their blood was on my hands now. I had written that code. I had pushed the button.

My responsibility.

The crashes grew fewer, and the shattering of glass became intermittent. I continued to perceive the passage of time in fits and starts.

Taking deep breaths, I got up from my chair, turned and walked out into the chapel. Most of the pews were overturned, fractured, splintered. The altar had been utterly pulverized. Bits of bread lay trampled flat on the ground, and a splatter of purple on the far wall hanging over a spray of glass shards marked where the chalice of wine had been thrown.

Father and Bogdan lay motionless on the floor near the altar, vacant stares in their eyes. A pool of blood had formed below Bogdan's head. I turned away. I thought momentarily that Timofei had escaped the carnage when I realized at the door it was his body I was stepping over.

I stepped out of the chapel's iris entrance and into the night. A glow had gone up from over the granary and a pyre had been ignited atop the dormitory, too. But the shouting and activity seemed to be coming from the Vestry Hall.

Slowly at first, with very careful, deliberate steps, I started toward it. It took every bit of effort to keep my thoughts focused. I remembered *War and Peace*, and all my conversations with Zhenya. I focused on that, and my steps grew swifter.

"Grisha?"

I turned and smiled. Andrei and Oleg walked slowly and deliberately toward me from the dormitory door.

"Guys?"

They held up their hands. "It's just us."

I held my own hands momentarily aloft. "You... we... did it."

"Yeah," Oleg confirmed. "We did."

All three of us frowned.

"What's... going on?" I asked. "They had me in the chapel the whole time."

"They've got the remaining Bishops," Oleg started.

"Artyom, Matvei, and Pavel, I think," Andrei interjected.

Oleg nodded. "Chained up in the Vestry Hall. They're crazy mad."

"I can't say I blame them. Do they know it was us?" I asked.

Andrei bit his lip, and Oleg looked at the ground.

"Guys?" I shook Andrei's shoulder.

"We just used the code you sent, and your sig was on the commits, so yeah, they... they've been chanting your name."

I closed my eyes and tried to absorb that. It didn't seem real. I clenched and unclenched my fists a few times. I breathed deeply and thought of Zhenya. And it hurt. Oh, how much those terrible moments hurt.

"Grisha." Oleg was shaking me by the shoulder. "We're here for you. Alright?"

I nodded. "Thank you." I grabbed both their shoulders and squeezed. "Thank you both."

I led them silently toward the Vestry Hall.

The Vestry Hall was filled with smoke, but through the haze

I could see an enormous glowing pile of vestments glowing red hot at the center, flames leaping toward the ceiling. I couldn't see the walls clearly, but I imagined they'd torn down every single scrum tapestry and set the pile of them alight.

At the edge of the pyre sat three figures, coughing and struggling. Figures stood around them holding blunt instruments that looked like legs of chairs or pieces of refectory tables. I spotted Brother Boris holding a curved pipe that had probably been torn out from under the refectory kitchen sink. About half had taken their robes off and wrapped them around their waist.

At the sight of me, the mob of them ran toward me. I held up my arms and Oleg and Andrei shouted at them, but they hauled me up onto their shoulders and drew me toward the pyre. I shouted to them to put me down, but all that came in response was the perpetual chant of my name: "Gri-go-ri, Gri-go-ri, Gri-go-ri."

They set me down atop a box before the three Bishops. They'd been gagged and they looked up at me with utter fear in their eyes. Tears, too, from all the smoke, but mostly fear. They struggled harder against their restraints. My brothers cheered.

Brother Boris handed me his pipe and a roar went up from the circle of seventy-odd monks. The cheering morphed into a chant of, "fi-nish them."

I held the pipe aloft.

The chanting grew louder and the cadence of the words faster.

I brought the pipe down in a swift stroke, and hurtled it into the pyre.

A victory cheer went up from the mob and died in a gasp.

"Give me a computer!" I shouted.

The mob mentality broken, individual monks started glancing about at one another.

"I said give me a computer!"

Some murmurs sounded, and finally Brother Boris stepped up toward me and handed me his computer. I logged in with my credentials, and reactivated the Vestry Hall's fire suppression system. The pyre dimmed and the smoke began evaporating as nanites scrubbed the air.

"This is over," I shouted. "No more killing."

"But they lied!" Someone shouted.

Shouts of, "liars," and "thieves" and "worse than bandits" went up from the crowd.

"No more killing!" I demanded. "We revoke their credentials and release them from the monastery."

Another chant started up. "Down with the monastery! Down with the Algorithm! No more deception!"

I shouted for them to listen, but it was some time before I could calm the crowd down from that one. Eventually I felt my voice was finally being heard. "Okay, so let's say we burn the monastery to the ground and destroy the repository. What then? Do we go back to our farms for the rest of our lives so our grandchildren can till a desert? Do we scatter our efforts and each try to solve the retracting habitability zone on our own? Do we join the bandits? Tell me, what's our long term plan for humanity?"

The room was silent.

"Well, I've got a plan. And it doesn't involve destroying the monastery. The Bishops lied to us because they were convinced that our environment couldn't be saved. I say they gave up too soon. We're software engineers. We can do better, and Yevgeny and I found books about how we can do that. Not everything they did in the Old World was wrong, and the idea of a perfect Algorithm isn't bad for us as long as we remember that it's an ideal we should strive for and not an idol to be worshipped blindly."

A monk in front knelt down on one leg and bowed his head. A second and third almost followed his lead, until I pointed at them and shouted, "Stand up! No, all of you, *stand up*! I will not be another Bishop. Not after what they did to Yevgeny. If we're going to do this, the office of Bishop is abolished. No more of them. Not now. Not ever. We're all brothers now. No more secrets and no more lies."

I extended my hand toward the monk who had knelt, Brother Lev, if memory served correctly. He looked at my hand, and looked at me, and then he took my hand in his. I stepped down off the box they'd set me on, shook his hand vigorously, and then did the same with each of my other brothers.

Our very first order of business was to isolate the Bishops' memory rewriting software and lock it down. The Brothers were divided on whether or not we should keep it or destroy it. We decided to keep it and teach every new initiate about how it was abused in the past, lest someone else try to write something similar. We also decided that no one in the monastery should have global access to all other Brothers' neural access keys. We each re-encrypted our own keys, deactivated those of the Bishops', along with the rest of their administrative access, and sent them packing.

We rebuilt the damaged parts of the granary first, then

the dorms and the refectory. The chapel remained a no man's land for many days.

I went there though, with Oleg and Andrei. I made sure that Father, Bogdan, and Timofei got a proper burial. Even afterwards, I would go and sit for many minutes at dawn every day in the front pew and look at the wrecked altar and broken glass. The names of the API method signatures were still there though. They'd been etched into the stone around the periphery of the windows—Create, Update, Generate, Delete, Alter, Reduce, Transform—on and on.

I started talking about *Working Effectively With Legacy Code* in small group sessions throughout the day. Those got more frequent and more intense as more monks started reading it.

Maxim, who'd spent the entirety of the catastrophe huddled in his chamber, finally came out of hiding. He silently joined my third *Legacy Code* lesson. I smiled at him, but he didn't smile back. At the end of the lesson, he asked if he could be entrusted to transcribe the book into digital form. I consented and by the next morning, he was done, and with a minimum of typos, too.

After that, my classes got going in a big way, and before long arguments were raging about the best way to isolate legacy behavior and put parts of the Holy Repository under test. The most heated arguments were over the old, forgotten feature requirements of the codebase, most of which had been lost since we no longer had the Bishops nor full recollection of every feature ever requested by them. Just because our memories had been restored didn't mean we were suddenly eidetic. Additional arguments broke out about which features were actually contributing to improvement and which had been part of the ruse.

One day, about two weeks in, after six consecutive *Legacy Code* sessions with my Brothers, Oleg came to my chamber. I almost asked him to come back in the morning, but it was Oleg, so I invited him in.

"There's one death we haven't taken care of," he said without even waiting for me to offer him a seat.

I searched my memory. We'd given all the dead Bishops proper burials. "Whose? I thought we got everyone."

Oleg bit his lip. "Someone whose death I'm worried you're avoiding dealing with."

For a few moments I thought only of Bishops, and then my brain skipped to the track Oleg had intended. I gulped and sadness welled up within me. And that terrible regret.

"I'm sorry," Oleg said. "I know you're busy. We're all really busy. But I think it's important for you."

"We—" I had to struggle to force out the words. "We—won't know—where the body is. And the Bishops are gone." Algorithm damn it, I was even tearing up.

"I had an idea about that," Oleg said. "Your place out in the forest. It was for the two of you, right?"

I nodded.

"Make that into the memorial. However you want. We could make that place really beautiful. That hike into the mountains is really nice. Anyway, it's just an idea. I just want you to have closure, and not get so busy now that you don't let yourself grieve. I think that'd be a mistake. My parents don't get to grieve over my brother. He's basically dead to us, and I saw how it ate at them." He stood up from his chair. "Anyway, sorry to butt in—"

"No," I said. "You're right. I think it's a good idea."

He gave me a weak smile. "Thanks."

I was glad he had brought it up, but I didn't sleep that night all the same, despite badly needing the rest. The next day I cancelled all my *Legacy Code* sessions and told Oleg, Maxim, and Andrei to pack up their things for a hiking trip after breakfast. By terce we were out the door and heading up into the mountain valley. Oleg, knowing full well what we were doing, lagged behind to explain to Maxim and Andrei in hushed tones.

"We're here for you, man," was all Andrei said along the way.

Maxim remained silent, while Oleg started in on ideas for a testing framework. I emailed him the stuff I'd been working on discreetly over the last week then and there.

"One thing though," Oleg said. "There was that other book. The story one. What was it?"

"*War and Peace*," I said.

"Right. It's clear how *Working Effectively With Legacy Code* is relevant for us, but what's with *War and Peace*? How come we're not reading that yet?"

"It's long and complex. It'll take time. We'll get there eventually, once testing is second nature."

"Is there some hidden message about coding better?" Andrei asked.

I shook my head. "No. It's about holiness, and what it means to be a good human being. It doesn't matter whether a religion has a daddy in the clouds, a perfect algorithm, or even something stupid, like, I don't know, a spaghetti monster. Anyone who tries to say that religion is bad because those things are irrational is missing the point. Those are supposed to be models for behavior. We all behave badly from time to time. We all screw up. The point is if you're not actively trying to be more compassionate, or more empathetic, or more intelligent, or more logical, more *something good*—basically, if you're not trying to make yourself a better human being, you're going to end up a worse human being. And that's why I knew I had to forgive even the people who destroyed the most beautiful part of my life. Because if I hadn't, I wouldn't have been human anymore. I'd have become just like them."

For a long time the only sounds were the birds and the wind and our footfalls crunching against the dirt.

"I'm sorry, you guys," Maxim said. "About... what I called you... before."

I turned and hugged him without hesitation. "It's all forgiven."

"Thank you," he said.

Not long after that we came to the clearing where the stairway to the underground door lay freely exposed. I came to a stop before it and pulled out my computer.

"We're here because I need to say goodbye to Yevgeny," I said. "I appreciate the way you guys covered for the two of us all these years, how we never stopped being friends even when it was clear what we were doing on our Days of Rest. We didn't have to feel like outcasts because of you guys, the way other monks definitely did. I know he appreciated that too.

"We're here also because I need to say I'm sorry. I have all this regret because of what I failed to do when he was alive. I could have insisted we go home together. I could have gone out looking for him the morning after I got back. I was just so scared of being targeted by monastery rules and traditions. I think part of the reason I want a new monastery is because I want to imagine that we can have the stability and the structure and the order without all the fear and prejudice. Maybe I'll just screw everything up as bad as the Bishops did. I don't know. But I want to try. And I think Zhenya would want that, too.

"I'm going to miss you Zhenya. I'm going to miss our talks. And especially our arguments. I'm going to miss the way you turned up the side of your mouth when you smiled, and the way you'd remind me to get my vestment done when I wanted to stay up late reading my favorite parts of *War and Peace*. I like how you challenged me to be a better programmer and a better human being.

"I'm going to miss you so much. Goodbye, Zhenya.

"Goodbye."

Monks and Code and Cats

an essay by the author

Ideas can come to writers anywhere and anytime. It is famous for those places to be incredibly inconvenient for the preservation and development of said ideas—places such as the shower—but, in my case, a compelling character or idea has a tendency to nag at me at least long enough for me to get access to a notepad or a computer. In the case of *Our Algorithm*, I was walking on the shore of Cannon Beach, Oregon near Haystack Rock with my husband. For whatever reason, Grisha and Zhenya and the Order of the Seventh Recursion came at me all at once and didn't let go. They were still with me when we got back to our hotel room. I grabbed up my computer and started writing straight away.

This novella was not the first time I had used a monastic setting in my writing, nor would it be the last. The short story *Temple of the Setting Sun* is set in a monastery in an Earth-like fantasy world. Earlier this year, I wrote and published the novella *Beati Qui Inveniunt Feles*, set in my new future-Earth history. And a yet-to-be published short story, *One's Own Medicine* is told from the perspective a monk on an alien Earth-like planet at their medieval stage of history.

I think that monasticism recurs in my work because the setting provides me a way to give my characters an environment where they must learn how to focus, to solve mysteries, to pay attention to the right details, to enact 'believing' in right and healthy ways as opposed to bad and unhealthy ones. If there is any common thread running through these four works, it is that of focus and attention to detail (critical skills for a software engineer, such as myself). I am not particularly enamored of rigid religious belief systems. However, I do find much of what I know of monastic life appealing, particularly the idea of structuring one's time to allow for the maximum application of focused attention against life's work.

And so I bend the rules of religion, something my chosen genres let me get away with. *Temple of the Setting Sun*'s invented religion is a Far East-inspired Zen-like fixation on color and shape. The monks of *Our Algorithm* worship a holy computer program, while those of *Beati Qui* worship pre-twenty-first century literature. So dedicated are they in protecting their library from infidels, that they genetically engineered a race of cyborg cats to serve as its protectors. The monks in *One's Own Medicine* are medical experts first and foremost; the details of their theological beliefs weren't necessary for the story. I'm pretty sure that by this point there remains not a real-life monastic order that would even consider me for membership (not that I'm particularly interested). Despite that, in a world that increasingly drives us to distraction every waking moment of our lives, that core idea of solitude and focus becomes more appealing for me year over year, which is why I think the monastic motif continues to pop up in my writing.

Our Algorithm is also interesting from the perspective of its role as a delineator in my development as a writer. I wrote this novella during October 2016, finishing its first draft a week before the United States presidential election of Donald Trump. Throughout 2016, I had been letting my publishing company, Fuzzy Hedgehog Press, limp along on life support. My business partner and I had gone separate ways in 2015, and I was left to manage everything alone. The election reshaped my understanding of the society I live in, and caused me to rethink my priorities; I chose to get my finances in order before dumping any more money into publishing. I shut down Fuzzy Hedgehog early in 2017 and spent a number of months figuring out the logistics of how I wanted to do publishing on the cheap while maintaining a minimum quality bar. I also discovered a love of Ancient Greek and Roman literature, which I explored for most of 2017 and 2018 before finally returning properly to writing.

This left a large gap in my writing output. By the time I returned to writing in 2019, I was a completely different person from the guy who penned *Our Algorithm* in 2016. The novella remains amongst my favorite works during that period, even more elegant in some ways than *Schrödinger's*

City, although the scale and scope of its world building is necessarily more limited. It is also a very personal story, in many ways a kind of love letter to my husband in the form of fiction, a way of thanking him for introducing me to so many of the beautiful works of Russian culture that I wouldn't have been exposed to otherwise.

I have no doubt that monastic orders will continue cropping up in my fiction for years to come. The details of what my monks pay attention to will undoubtedly continue to vary—colors, code, cats, cholera—but that fact of paying attention, of engaging deeply, of dedication, both intellectual and emotional, is likely to remain constant. This world will continue to pull me in a many directions at once. What good would a genre be if it wasn't capable of helping me to imagine something different?

— Matthew Buscemi
Seattle, November 2020

www.ingramcontent.com/pod-product-compliance
Lightning Source LLC
Chambersburg PA
CBHW030606130626
46552CB00006B/2681